CURTAINS

ALSO BY

DREW THOMAS:

<u>LONDON LEGENDS SERIES</u>

Weird Sex

What A Performance

<u>THE GRASS IS ALWAYS GREENER SERIES</u>

The Hairdresser's Tale

The Baroness's Tale

The Publican's Tale

The Skipperess's Tale

www.drewthomasworld.com

CURTAINS

DREW THOMAS

CHERWELL

A CHERWELL PAPERBACK

First published in Great Britain in 2012 by

Cherwell Books

Copyright © Drew Thomas 2012

The right of Drew Thomas to be identified as the author of this work has been asserted by him in accordance with the Copyright, Designs and Patents Act of 1988.

No part of this publication may be reproduced, stored in a retrieval system, or transmitted in any form or by any means, electronic, mechanical, photocopying, recording, or otherwise, without the prior permission of the copyright owner.

This is a work of fiction. All characters, organizations and events portrayed in this novel are either products of the author's imagination or are used fictitiously.

Cover design by Damonza

A CIP catalogue record for this title is available from the British Library

ISBN 978-0-9571878-0-1

Cherwell Books

www.cherwellbooks.com

This novel is dedicated to the gift of sight

All author royalties earned from
the sale of this book will be donated to
VISION AID OVERSEAS,
a charity working to transform access to
eye care services for people in developing countries.

www.vao.org.uk

This gift of mimicry in the actor is like a gift for likeness in a painter. Such a knack will not make his drawing fine, but it will give him a kind of solid reality which he can begin with and which he can alter and force to his own ends.

Stark Young (1881-1963)

The Meeting

E

I haven't set foot outside for so long that I've probably had too much time to prevaricate over the best place to begin my story. You could be forgiven for thinking that you already know the facts since the sordid details of the case were extensively recorded in the tabloids, but – as is often the case – the reported train of events and the truth have little in common with each other. Hasn't it been said that the history of a war – and I am not exaggerating when I describe the happenings of nearly three years ago as such – is invariably written by the victor? And I allowed my wife, at least for a while, to believe that she had beaten me.

Bearing this in mind, I suppose it is inevitable that I find myself drawn to the night I first met her. Since you will have heard or read at least some of her proclamations that she was the sole architect of my fame, I hope it will suffice as a beginning. Whether it does or not, I feel the need, for the sake of my sanity, to begin this very personal memoir immediately – before the future becomes the present and the present becomes the past. Even the recent past is a fragile entity, more than a little at the mercy of memory.

'Hurry up or I'm going to pee myself!' Venomous and filled with urgency, they were the first words she ever spoke to me that night almost eleven years ago. I suppose I must have felt it bristling about her – that quality that is either impressive, terrifying or both: the desire for fame. Did I have it myself? I really don't know. I certainly didn't know back then. It's too easy to adjust and re-adjust remembered happenings, let alone thoughts and feelings. I do know that it was a dangerous game I was playing when I left myself behind as I went through the curtains and put every ounce of available energy into that macabre tennis match with the audience, terrified as I launched each volley that it wouldn't come back, but rarely disappointed.

We were backstage in a scruffy little South London cabaret pub, which has since been romanticized as the birthplace of more than one show business personality to save it from being knocked down to make way for, in turn, a leisure centre and a German supermarket. I was there simply because it was on my circuit: one of the venues in which I could come alive in front of an audience. Strangely enough, nobody has joined the dots and identified that pub as my launch pad, but I suppose I was a very different being in those days.

Roni took the raw potential she found and, after pounding it down as if it were clay, remoulded, reworked and re-branded it into the star material she was to treat as her property. Even when – eight years later – The Shooting was headline news and there was an unbelievable demand for any snippet of gossip about me, no journalist traced the beginnings of my career back to that pub. No footage from those early days exists.

I hadn't long finished my act and was trying to get out of the filthy lavatory without grasping the greasy doorknob too tightly for fear of its incumbent germs being transferred to my hand. 'Hurry up or I'm going to pee myself!' There she was, white blonde hair teased into wisps around her face, her lithe body sheathed in a purple bugle beaded gown, glaring at me like a ferocious she-tiger. 'Now!' Smoke from the Sobranie Black Russian clamped between her carmine lips wafted into my face. Veronica Bedford. Roni for short. On stage in less than two minutes and clearly desperate to use the slimy grey convenience I was doing my best to vacate.

She was a mesmerizing splash of raw sinewy colour against the drab backstage corridor. I'd seen her name on the posters and heard a septuagenarian drag artiste warning a lesbian saxophonist that she wasn't to be messed with, so you can understand I was a little apprehensive. She yanked the door open with a hand sporting glossy purple nails, causing me to stumble and fall face down on the filthy grey linoleum. The chrome dove pan I had been carrying clattered to the floor ahead of me. A gold stiletto heel narrowly missed my face as she hoisted up the shimmering dress around her thighs with one hand and pulled the door shut with the other. I picked myself up and raised my eyebrows to nobody in particular, then stooped to recover the dove pan.

One of the most popular magic props in the business, the dove pan looks like a chrome serving dish with a large domed lid. The plate is empty. The lid is also apparently empty. You pour paraffin onto the plate and ignite it with a flourish, hopefully without setting fire to any curtains like I did the first time I tried it at home.

Home at the time was a little rented flat in Battersea – the first place I had really ever thought of as my own home. Although it came furnished, I added a bit of my own style: thick black chenille curtains with broad sashes of rope in the bedroom and, in the small living room, unbleached calico lashed to a heavy ash pole with rough hemp cord threaded through large brass eyelets in the fabric covering the whole of one wall. I've seen the idea since in magazines, but I know I thought of it first, unless curtain fashions are simultaneously spontaneous, like playground rhymes. (Apparently, children as far apart as Australia, South Africa and Scotland were, within days of each other, singing versions of the same ditty about the use of cocaine 'recited with little understanding but enthusiastic actions'. Who on earth does the research to come up with facts like these?)

Next door but one there lived an old lady who used to lean out of her window to complain loudly about her young upwardly-mobile neighbours parking their car on the pavement. She wouldn't be able to get out of her gate, she said. I soon found out that she never went out anyway. I admired that – the fact that she was content never to leave her territory.

I was just putting the key in my front door on one of the occasions she was giving a verbal lashing to Roger and Samantha or Benjamin and Annabel or whatever they were called, when she turned her gaze towards me – her violet crushed velvet housecoat open enough to reveal a glimpse of a flowered winceyette nightdress underneath – and said pointedly that she liked the look of me and asked if I would like to come in for a cup of tea.

I didn't know what exactly had taken her fancy, but was flattered. Her apparent lack of concern with her appearance intrigued me. I took a deep breath and politely accepted her invitation. The tea didn't materialize, not that day anyway, as she was too preoccupied with introducing me to her world: a world of variety acts and showgirls, magicians and tap dancers, mime artistes and ventriloquists. The evidence was there in the faded and tattered posters taped to the grubby wallpaper of Iris Devereux's parlour. I couldn't get the questions out fast enough. Had she been a performer? What had she done? Where had she worked? Whom had she worked with?

'We're not here to talk about my life. It's nearly over now Daniel,' she said, 'or can I call you Danny? Tell me about you.' Temptation overcame my bashfulness and I suddenly found myself in the middle of telling – or rather showing – her my life story, punctuated with a stream of visitors and guests, including Stella, who sprang to vibrant and verbose life in order to meet my new acquaintance. Iris didn't seem remotely perturbed by her brazenness. In fact, she openly encouraged her.

'She's a corker, Danny,' she cackled when Stella had gone. 'Characters like that don't come easy.'

'I'm still not sure where she came from,' I said in all sincerity. Iris gave me one of her sideways glances – a look with which I was to become very familiar. 'In fact,' I told her, 'I'm not sure where any of them came from.' It took a moment or two for the truth of this self-revelation to sink in.

'Danny my boy, it's a gift not to be sniffed at!' She leaned forward and put her withered face close to mine. I could smell lily of the valley talcum powder and a memory of something like musk. 'You've been hiding your light under a bushel for too long. You need to let them out more.'

'All of them?' I asked incredulously.

'Of course,' she said sagely, tapping her forehead. I felt Stella's stirrings of approval deep inside me as the old lady chortled on. 'There I was thinking nobody wanted to do a proper act any more, and along you come into my life.'

I knew that she was genuinely pleased to have met me and wanted to give her something in return. She had a glint in her yellowed but still sparkling eyes as I launched into a brand new dialogue that featured Marlene Dietrich telling the Queen Mother that it had taken more than one man to change her name to Shanghai Lily.

It wasn't until a later visit that I surprised myself by divulging the secret that I was still a virgin and went on to explain that it was largely as a result of Stella's frequently recounted sexual activities filling me with a fascinated disgust. Before long, in fact, I found that I had come to rely on Iris. She was a complete audience embodied in one woman. With the slightest lift of an eyebrow or the tiniest hint of a smile forming on her sagging lips, she gave me more useful feedback than I got from a cheering audience of two hundred in a smoky pub.

One thing led to another and she presented me with the dove pan, which – after a bit of practice and the sacrifice of fifteen metres of unbleached calico – I soon mastered. When I'd managed to track down and train some doves – slender Barbaries with snow white feathers and delicate red legs – the dove pan was occasionally in my act, much to Stella's dismay. She didn't like the new character who operated it: a transsexual magician with a nifty line in double entendre. I was cheapening the act, she said. Who was Stella to talk but a fictitious foul-mouthed butcher's wife with bleached hair, ginger roots and a talent for singing off key?

So, after the plate is ignited, the raging inferno is extinguished with the shiny domed lid, which is then lifted up and – hey presto! – the doves appear as if by magic and flutter prettily around the stage. And that was why I was in the greasy grey lavatory on that fateful night – to empty the paraffin and petrol mixture from the bottom of my dove pan. Well, where else was I going to get rid of it? And was it my fault that it didn't flush properly, leaving the flammable liquid floating on the surface of the water? It didn't occur to me that Roni would drop her lit cigarette between her legs. Her piercing yell cut through the urine-scented atmosphere (now tinged with the aroma of burning hair) before I'd got to my feet. 'I know who you are! I'll see you later!'

I collected my props, costumes, wigs and doves and vacated the premises in record time as her words rang in my ears: a threat and promise that would change my life for ever.

My act had gone down well that night, so I didn't really dwell on the incident with the paraffin for long. To say it was 'my' act would be slightly misleading. As I saw it, I hosted an hour or so on stage with a selection of my 'guests' – some drawn from real life, others fictitious – who came as if from nowhere to join me. Iris was right about the fact that I didn't realize mimicry was such a talent until it dawned on me that not everyone could do it. I was no stranger to the fact that it was difficult and emotionally draining, but I'd thought that most people just didn't *want* to do it.

The unfortunate episode with the blonde singer (for that's all Roni was to me at that point) would probably have faded from my memory entirely before long. Even though it was a comic moment, that kind of thing is usually only funny at the time it happens and not worth storing as potential material. Life went on day by day, night by night, and featured, I distinctly remember, the sudden arrival in a pub on the Old Kent Road of Eartha Kitt doing a startling version of 'Morning Has Broken'.

Anyway, near the end of a long night that had included an exhausting booking at a private stag night, I was doing a late slot at a notorious gay club in the East End. I was half way through a heartbreakingly tearful rendition of Judy Garland doing 'Over the Rainbow' – which I must admit took me almost as much by surprise as it clearly did the audience – when I spotted the dove pan blonde at the back of the crowd. She was staring straight at me and, no matter what – or whom – I did, I couldn't escape that piercing gaze. By the end of my set, which overran somewhat due to an unexpected argument about reflected glory between Liza Minelli and Lorna Luft, I could still see her there at the back and was completely convinced – although not afraid – that she had come to get me.

She had. And I now know that I should have been afraid.

She cornered me as I came out of the dressing room. It was difficult enough trying to carry two large suitcases and three wigs on stands (thankfully I hadn't got the doves that night) without a fiery determined blonde in stiletto-heeled boots, black leather jeans and a scarlet cashmere jersey, which I couldn't help but notice matched the shade of her lipstick perfectly, trying to block my way. I contemplated apologizing for the dove pan incident, then thought about pretending I didn't remember her. It did occur to me for a fleeting second that she might be insane. I opened my mouth to say something, although I can't for the life of me imagine what it was going to be, but she spoke first.

'You're wasting your talent.'

'I beg your pardon?' It wasn't the best retort I could have come up with, but her words had taken me by surprise.

'Let me give you a hand with those.' She took one of the suitcases from me and, before I could object, was propelling me outside towards a waiting cab. 'I've been watching you. We need to talk.'

'Do we?' I could hear myself becoming more imbecilic by the moment.

'I take it you're gay?' She took the other suitcase from me and hurled it into the cab as I clutched my wigs protectively to my chest.

'No!' I don't know why, but it came out very emphatically.

'No?' She blinked and looked at me as if for the first time. Her eyes opened wider and her hitherto tight red lips loosened into a smile.

The memory of it still bewilders me. One minute we were outside a scruffy East End pub, then less than half an hour later we were sitting comfortably in a quiet corner of a private club in Soho, my suitcases and wigs safely stashed in the cloakroom. Roni was extolling my virtues – or at least the virtues of my act – telling me that she'd been watching me closely for the past two weeks and thought my potential was largely untapped. I hated myself for it, but I was flattered. Above all, though, I was relieved, because I had thought she was coming after me to wreak revenge.

She knew my act, virtually knew my entire repertoire, knew all the places in which I worked and – most significantly of all – offered her services as my manager. I laughed. The concept of me having a manager was funny. And as if that wasn't amusing enough, the person offering to be that manager was a blonde cabaret singer who had only taken notice of me because I'd caused her to singe her private parts in a dreary pub toilet in Vauxhall.

By the end of that evening, assisted by the contents of several bottles, Roni had done her best to persuade me that her proposition could possibly be an extremely good idea – one that made perfect sense in the precarious profession in which I had found myself.

At the time I met Roni, I was living a rather strange existence in that I can't remember feeling much except when I was on stage. My mother had died six months earlier from a massive stroke, an event that filled me with a sadness that was actually the realization of a feeling of loss that had been gradually building for many years, but the real source of this numbness was the more recent death of my old friend and mentor Iris Devereux.

Iris died peacefully in her sleep amidst the tatty but comfortable surroundings that had become her whole life – or at least the physical boundaries of it. She may never have left her home in the time that I knew her, but she was with me in spirit every time I waited to go on stage. Her chuckles, sniggers, hearty laughs and stern admonitions were always ringing in my ears. She was the nearest I'd ever come to having a rehearsal audience. She was the one who eased the painful birth of new routines, the one who knew when I was on the right track and when I most definitely wasn't. 'Knock it on the head for now and put the kettle on, Danny boy,' she would cackle, 'though God knows it won't suit you!'

Without causing offence, because I recognized and respected the fact that she had the privilege of the old and experienced of freely saying what she thought, she could completely annihilate a routine I'd been working on for weeks, then help me form another around a grain of wit she could identify as having 'possibilities, Danny boy, possibilities.' She gave me so much and made me allow her to give it because she had the gift of being able to make it appear that I was giving her more in return.

We were quite a team.
And then she died.

I can remember every set of curtains I've ever waited behind. I can remember which ones were before Iris died and which ones were after. And which ones were after Roni had come into my life.

'How do you do it? How?' Roni's eyes sparkled as she listened to my unrehearsed rendition of Maria Callas doing a current Kylie Minogue number. She was the first visitor to my Battersea flat since I'd lived there. 'Don't tell me you just launch into it and it happens. I wasn't born yesterday!' She laughed delightedly and clapped her hands together. 'You can be honest with me.'

It has since been said that I never wrote my own material. Someone even came up with the bizarre notion that Roni wrote the scripts and I was just her front man, her puppet. These stories ought to annoy me, but as a safeguard against that I have every single script and performance note that I wrote – along with numerous recordings of live performances I did – after Roni became my manager. I've carefully filed and classified them. I could find any of them within minutes. They are artfully stored on twenty five and a half square metres of shelving hidden behind floor to ceiling ivory damask curtains in my study. Illuminated from behind, since there is no natural light when the door is closed, I can adjust the lights to imitate any time of day or night, creating the illusion that it's morning, noon or a moonlit night. It looks like a curtained window, but it's my early mainstream career.

I rarely feel the need to search through it, but I know it's there if I want to.

'Just be yourself,' Roni was to say before long, once she'd gained my trust. 'Just be yourself and let it flow. You don't need all those gimmicks and voices to hide behind.' Little did she know.

It's comforting to have windows, although there aren't any in my study. I say 'my' study, but really it's Roni's. The whole place is Roni's. From the huge windows in the main split level 'living space' (as you can't seem to call a room a room, a flat a flat or even a house a house these days), I have a wide uninterrupted view of the river Thames. It's like having my own personal soap opera populated with characters who don't know they're being watched. It has been a great comfort to me as, until last night, I hadn't seen anyone face to face since my incarceration began.

There's a small tugboat I see frequently going one way or the other, sometimes on its own, sometimes pulling or pushing huge barges laden with containers. Through my telescope I can see that the same man drives it each time. Maybe he owns it. Maybe it's his life or, more likely, it's his livelihood, supporting his life. Perhaps he has a wife, possibly children. I like to think that he chose this way of life above all others. I will never know and am aware that things are very rarely as they seem. But I still like to watch as the tugboat propels or hauls its various burdens up and down the river with its helmsman completely oblivious to my avid observation and speculation.

There are many other boats too, but none that fascinates me like that one. Even the Royal Yacht Britannia on its final visit to London failed to arouse in me any feelings at all – probably because that was precisely what it was designed and built to do.

Is that what I was designed and built to do?

'Just be yourself,' Roni said.

Difficult as it may be, I am going to force myself to start getting ready three hours before tonight's Night Delivery is due. The frequent daytime deliveries are different. I open the street door when they buzz on the intercom and get them to leave the boxes and crates inside. My regular man who delivers the groceries shouts a deferential 'Thank you Madam' up the stairs before shutting the door behind himself. It still amuses me that he believes he is delivering to the woman he can picture behind the voice. For a Night Delivery, however, I need to see them in person and they obviously need to see me, even though it's not me they see – if you get my drift – which is why it takes me three hours to get ready.

This is the second one, so I'm getting the hang of it, but in no way am I complacent. Complacency leads to carelessness. Carelessness leads to failure. To go on stage feeling fully prepared and entirely capable of doing what you are meant to be doing is a sure recipe for disaster. There has to be apprehension and insecurity and more than a hint of fear.

The fear, however unpleasant, is essential.

For tonight, I have chosen an outfit that is exceedingly uncomfortable – a sheath dress in turquoise shot silk cut on the bias with a ribbed, embroidered bodice. It's an old ploy to keep me on my toes and remind me of the dangers. If all goes to plan, of course, it doesn't matter how my visitor sees me – or at least what he sees – but I have to prepare for every eventuality. Maybe, although I scare myself by even thinking about it, I yearn for the unexpected.

Everything I need is either hanging up in the dressing room or laid out on Roni's dressing table, including a bottle of ink, a needle and the letter 'E', carefully and decoratively copied onto crisp white cartridge paper from a King James Bible printed in 1947 I found at a car boot sale in Croydon several weeks before the Big Break. During those three hours I sit, great swathes of floor-to-ceiling indigo linen hanging on either side of the mirror, and look at the face looking back at me as it changes.

Is a man who chooses when to die more or less in control of his destiny than one who waits for death to take him by surprise?

The Early Courtship

R

'So come on. Tell me how you started.' Roni put her hand on my knee and looked at me with the appealing green eyes I could imagine opening doors and securing favours. 'With the act I mean.' I really didn't know where to begin, but I thankfully didn't have to as she continued excitedly. 'It's so unique, so daring! The impressions... the mimicry... how did you start?' We were in a small restaurant in Clapham Old Town with rough wooden tables, hard benches, dog-eared menus and brusque French staff who appeared to care more for the pungent shellfish they served than for their customers. I had just done a show in an old style cabaret pub down the road and – although I hadn't yet agreed to let her manage me – had willingly allowed her to take charge of ordering. 'What do you think of the wine?' She looked at me and betrayed the first hint of an eagerness to please.

'It's great,' I said once I'd tasted it – a rustic earthy Gamay, which conjured up vivid but improbable images of peasant workers gathering grapes in wicker baskets on their backs – glad of the excuse to avoid answering her other questions.

'I *knew* you'd like it!' Her confidence seemed to be infectious and – before long – I found that I was impressed with everything she did, from the way she dealt with the forbidding staff to her knowledge of the menu and apparent instinct to know what I would enjoy. 'You're looking more comfortable than you were when we first came in.' She was right; I felt strangely at ease and was even beginning to enjoy myself.

'Well, you know, I don't really socialize much.' The truth was that I didn't socialize at all.

'I find that hard to believe,' she grinned as she topped up my glass, 'coming from a man with such a sparkling wit and knack for sprightly repartee.' I didn't know how to reply to this, so didn't. I took comfort from the fact that she didn't know me and was mistaken in expecting me to perform even when I wasn't on stage. That comfort, coupled with the warm euphoria induced by the wine, helped me to relax and I started to feel a creeping fascination with this woman who had sought me out.

'So how did you get into this business?' It seemed like the right question to ask. I desperately wanted to keep the conversation flowing.

'You don't want to know about *my* life, surely?' she asked rhetorically, moving aside a fraction to allow a waiter to place two steaming bowls of mussels on the table. 'I'm sure I'm nothing unusual.' I knew that she knew that wasn't true, even as she waved a well-manicured hand in a casually dismissive gesture. 'I was the only child of a single mother who resented the downturn her musical career took when I was born.'

'Your mother was a singer?'

'A musical actress. She chose to blame her failure to succeed on my arrival in the world.'

'Parents can be cruel.'

'She died.' Roni paused and I glimpsed a barely perceptible but nonetheless frightening hardness in her expression. 'I'd been spotted by an agent playing Sandy in an amateur youth production of *Grease*. It led to a national tour and all kinds of possibilities.' Her gaze wandered over my right shoulder for a moment, then she shifted her focus back to my face. 'That's when I became Veronica Bedford,' she said with a self-deprecating frown. 'I was born Barbara Unwin, which wasn't a name I could envisage in lights, emblazoned across marquees in the West End.' The laugh that accompanied this admission was tainted with a barely detectable hollowness. 'Can you imagine?' I *could* imagine. My heart went out to this eager girl full of optimism, drive and enthusiasm. 'Anyway, listen to me going on about myself!'

'Don't stop!' My words came out rather loudly as I clumsily reached out to put my hand over hers, then changed my mind and took it back. A strange thing was happening to me that I could feel but not explain. 'I mean, what happened next?'

'Not enough.' A brief, high-pitched laugh escaped her lips. She sounded deflated rather than bitter. 'Three years at LAMDA honing my voice, my acting skills, learning how to use what I had.' She looked straight at me and I still, to this day, don't think the tear in the corner of one of her eyes was a figment of my imagination. There was more than a hint of self-loathing in this seemingly confident young woman. At thirty two she was more than five years older than I was and desperately in need of success and recognition. I saw her suddenly in a different light, saw that her slim figure was the result of constant dieting and working out, that the apparently confident demeanour was the product of similar excruciatingly hard work and that – beneath it all – she was possibly as afraid of the world as I was.

She went on to expound her theory that the musical theatre didn't make stars any more, coupled with the fact that there were no new quality musicals being written. 'I could add that I was always too young, short, slim or angular for the available parts, but I won't. So now I traipse around the cabaret circuit belting out the songs from the shows.' The pause that followed was on the verge of becoming poignant when her smile suddenly returned. 'But now *you've* come into my life!' She clapped her hands together and laughed again, but this time the twinkle was back in her eyes.

My heart lurched and I began to feel – without having to question it – that my life had begun. Here was a situation in which I was involved, rather than sensing its potential for enjoyment but being distanced from it. By the end of the evening, it seemed a natural progression that Roni would – from that moment on – be my manager.

'What have you got to lose?' she asked.
What had I got to lose?

Stella likes to think of herself as an undiscovered cockney Marlene Dietrich. I think of her as a bloody nuisance who has frequently led me to believe that I am losing my mind. From the moment of her first appearance, when she erupted into my life like a newly-awakened volcano, I knew that she was different from any of the others and was afraid of her. This fear was somewhat allayed – at least for a while – by the enthusiasm Iris showed for her. It was Iris who encouraged Stella to expand upon her past, never using the words 'fabricate' or 'falsify' in this context. 'Tell us where you were born, Stella love,' she would say, chuckling to herself in anticipation.

As a result, we learned about Stella's childhood as the illegitimate daughter of a Jewish pub singer from Stepney and a Roman Catholic priest, a childhood largely spent begging, stealing and borrowing which led, in turn, to teenage years spent working in a Soho club as a hostess before an ill-advised marriage to a butcher from Bermondsey. 'Give us a song, lovely,' Iris would cackle, 'give us a song.' Stella couldn't sing, but that didn't stop her. 'Now that's what I call a song!' Iris used to have tears of mirth running down her cheeks by the time Stella had finished and I'd got my breath back.

'She's your future, Danny boy,' she said one day when Stella had retreated. 'Keep her in order and she'll see you into your retirement.' Maybe she was right.

'Why are you letting that little upstart change your act?' Stella's words were filled with venom and I felt the mixture of fear and loathing I usually did when she appeared. The day before, Roni had said bluntly that Stella was nothing more than a character on which I fell back when I couldn't come up with anything else. 'It's your act. Do it your way!' She didn't seem to realize that I didn't have the power to decide when Stella would appear.

And when she did, she frightened me.

My old cabaret routines in the Early Days relied heavily on my ability to lose control – or at least surrender control to a series of personae that were themselves controlled by the demands of the audience. Rehearsal was almost as impossible as predicting how the routine would run, but I knew what I was doing. This, I thought, was the way it would continue. Roni, I thought, loved what I did. I could be forgiven for thinking this since she cleverly told me so on several occasions.

My decision to take her on as my manager, which I later realized was not my decision at all, was immediately followed by her proving that she was more than capable of rising to the challenge.

'I've got three bookings on Friday night, two on Saturday and a Sunday lunchtime!' She was standing on my doorstep waving her leather bound desk diary and looking very pleased with herself. Her face suddenly fell. She must have detected some panic in my expression. 'My God, Danny, I'm sorry. I should have rung to make sure you could manage that many. Shall I—'

'No!' I must have sounded desperate, but I wanted her to smile again. 'That's brilliant Roni.'

'Are you sure?' She creased her brow and put her hand on my wrist. 'You only have to say.'

'Of course I'm sure.' I forced a bright smile, hoping to see its reflection in her features. 'I'll put the kettle on,' I added lamely, stepping back to let her in.

'It won't suit you.' She lifted her face and grinned wickedly from beneath her newly-coiffed bob.

She took to the role of manager like a duck to water; she had the drive, ambition and sheer pushiness to sell what I did. I can't deny that she secured more bookings in our first year together than I would have dared to imagine were possible. She was my back-up. She was behind me all the way. She believed in me unconditionally.

Or so she allowed me to think.

It would be easy for me to pretend – or pretend to remember – that my working relationship with Stella took a turn for the worse when Roni came into my life, but the truth of the matter is that she had never been easy to work with.

My signature impersonation in the Early Days – although I never thought of it as that – was Dusty Springfield's 'You Don't Have To Say You Love Me'. It became something for which the audience at my regular bookings would shout and scream and, as a result, something I couldn't avoid. But it always left me drained, tired and tearful. I could feel Dusty's pain and hurt as if it were my own and always tried to leave the number as an encore.

Stella once – and only once – did a cruel rendition of the song, parodying the tragedy and heartache. What made it worse was that she poked fun at my sincere tears, implying that I was just milking the audience for sympathy, pulling their heart strings using cheap gimmicks.

'Does he really think it's worth shedding crocodile tears for a tortured lesbian?' Her words were genuinely spiteful. 'For God's sake don't humour him any more by pretending you care. Now let me show you a real song!' With that she launched into a quite filthy version of 'Love For Sale'.

It was obvious that she realized she had done wrong, even though her delight at the reaction from the audience was almost palpable, because she actually apologized to me in the dressing room afterwards. As if that wasn't enough, she also assured me that she wouldn't do it again, but – while it takes me a long time to get angry – it takes me even longer to forgive. Any remnant of trust and confidence I had in Stella vanished that day. Our relationship was never to be the same again. I would like to say that I would have stood up to her even if Roni hadn't been there to back me up. On the other hand, I am trying to make this memoir an honest account.

'Excellent! I *told* you that Bette Midler bit would work. Develop more stuff like that and we'll be filling theatres before long.' I should have admired Roni's ambition and optimism when she said things like that. Instead I imagined curtains. Huge sinister curtains waiting to open. 'But only if it feels right for you, of course,' she added hastily, having clearly interpreted my apprehensive expression correctly.

'I think you might be jumping ahead a bit too fast,' I said nervously, feeling the need to concentrate on what I was doing. We were rehearsing – in as much as that was possible – for a booking at a Bar Mitzvah that night. It was a lucrative gig but the demands had been very specific.

'Sorry Danny.' Her laugh reverberated around my little living room in a clear attempt to lighten the mood. 'You mustn't let me forget it's your act. You know what a pushy cow I can be.'

'Please don't think I'm ungrateful.' I could feel Stella waking up and wasn't in the mood for her tactless interference. My mind went suddenly blank and I looked at Roni, the first tinges of panic beginning to take hold. What if this happened in the middle of the performance? Having to structure the act so rigidly had thrown me off balance. 'So what comes next?'

'Barbra Streisand,' Roni said calmly and rubbed her hands together in anticipation. 'They're going to love her!' Seeing the belief she had in me, I felt myself relax.

What was more important was that, for the first time ever, I had been able to keep Stella at bay.

There was always method to Roni's actions. While confident that she would be able to make me into a commercial sensation, she found herself faced with a couple of challenges. The first was to find how to tempt me with success, when I was neither interested in nor impressed by the rewards it could offer. The second was how to ensure that she was a permanent fixture in my life.

It wasn't long before she had identified an ingenious way to conquer that second challenge.

Like the feeling of overwhelming relief and sense of recognition induced by the discovery of a divine story by someone who desperately needs to believe in something, my love for Roni crept up on me at first like an unwelcome visitor, then like a warm cloud enveloping me in a benevolent, trust-filled haze that softened, heightened and coloured all I saw and did. Not since my early childhood – during the years before my mother's accident when she used to wrap me in a big, soft orange towel after my bath and sit me on her knee – had I felt such seemingly unconditional love, unexplained and inexplicable.

I found myself looking at Roni's individual features – the curve of her top lip, the lobe of her right ear, a small mole just above the hairline on her left temple – and seeing them as if for the first time, but also as if they had been part of my life for ever. The way she put her index finger, its nail always immaculately varnished, to her chin when she was deep in contemplation fascinated me. More than anything, I longed to see the birth and development of her every smile when it was as a result of approval at a routine I had adjusted for her. It was not unlike the appreciation I both sought and needed from an audience, but Roni's endorsement gave me the confidence to grow and flourish in a manner that was at first disconcerting.

Once I had allowed myself to believe that she really liked what I did – that she really liked *me* – it tinted my existence with a favourable blush and even began to eradicate the cynicism on which I had come to rely so heavily. I wanted to impress her. I needed to impress her. In fact, I don't think I'm exaggerating when I say that I actually ached to please her. The most notable point in all this – as far as I can see – is that I was actually optimistic that I could achieve these newfound desires.

What made this renaissance more remarkable was that, up until that point, I had assumed and even come to rely on the fact that I would live my private life in solitude. It is possible that I had carefully conditioned myself to think this way in order to avoid disappointment and protect what I knew was my inherent delicate sensibility. Roni's subsequent unsolicited arrival had been a complete bolt from the blue. As a result, I felt as if I had been reborn, or at least as if rebirth was possible. I told myself that if the love I felt for Roni could be reciprocated and take a physical as well as cerebral form, my life – and indeed our lives together – would be complete.

It sounds crass and clichéd now after all that has happened, but I know without a shadow of a doubt that these sentiments were very real to me at the time. If they hadn't been, my life might have taken a very different course and I wouldn't be sitting here writing this.

In the Early Days, before I met Roni, variety wasn't a luxury, but rather a dangerously uncontrollable force in my life. In itself, it didn't rule my existence, but the attempts to control it did. I mean 'variety' as in the old Heinz label, but I suppose, now I think about it, the other type – as in 'Leeds City Varieties' – aptly describes my career at that point. I occasionally have a fanciful notion that I didn't know what I was doing, even though I know that wasn't the case. I knew perfectly well what I was unleashing every time I stepped onto a stage in front of an audience.

I had a solid base of failsafe material from which I worked, allowing me the freedom to let my act take me on a journey. At any time, however far from it my on-stage meanderings had taken me, I could dart back to it and be safe. Knowing that I had something to turn to, something to draw on, helped me to soar with the spontaneity of the moment, like an eagle being carried on currents of air high in the sky. I later referred to it as my 'tree' method – the failsafe material forming the trunk and the spontaneous meanderings the branches, twigs, leaves and, occasionally, blossoms. Rather than working in a tree, though, in the Early Days it was more like working in a forest or jungle. It was a fight for survival.

Isn't that what life needs to be in order to be fulfilling?

'Yes!' Roni squealed with glee, hugged me and put a large glass of wine in my hand. 'I have a feeling the Barbra cookery spot is going to stay in the act from now on.' The Bar Mitzvah audience had cheered, clapped and laughed for the entire hour and a half I had been on stage. I was slumped in a chair in the tiny dressing room, exhausted and speechless.

Looking back to those times, I realize that her methods were systematic. Once she had decided a piece was coming out of the routine, it would come out. Once she had decided I should try something new, I tried it. This was obviously quite a task for her, since not even I knew what was definitely in or out of the act until it had actually happened.

I now appreciate how much easier her task was after she had worked out how to make me fall in love with her.

No matter how well engineered it is, to be successful an act must appear to come together effortlessly.

This evening, the food delivery man arrived bang on time as usual. His breezy 'Thank you Madam' filtered up the stairs just before I heard the door slam shut. I was able to get dinner ready straight away, leaving plenty of time to prepare for tonight's visitor. I have been here in front of the mirror for almost an hour already. The lights around the mirror illuminate my face, which is itself reflected in the mirror. Any transformation has to come from the inside out. Nothing can materialize without having first been planned and pieced together. This apartment is a good example, since it only became a reality because of my ability to put ideas into practice. Admittedly, Roni found and acquired the property, or properties, through her pushiness and inability to take no for an answer. She found the raw material – the skeleton if you like – but I put flesh on the bones and brought this space to life. And now I'm sitting in it, in front of a mirror, preparing myself for what could be called a performance. My whole life has been a seemingly interminable series of performances.

I have just heard on the radio – a medium that has never intimidated me the way television has – that a body has been pulled out of the river at the Thames Barrier. There are, apparently, several bodies pulled out of or washed up on the banks of the Thames every week, but few of them are worthy of the news. This one is that of a young male, found naked with no distinguishing marks except for a decorative 'V' newly tattooed on his chest. It has made the news because it is thought that it might be connected to the discovery of the headless and limbless torso of an African child found in the river some months ago, which was the source of much speculation about ritual human sacrifice. I am the only one who knows categorically that it isn't connected.

A pair of black leather jeans and a scarlet cashmere jersey are hanging on one of the wardrobe doors behind me. The stiletto-heeled boots that complete the outfit are on the floor at my feet. An array of make-up, including a scarlet lipstick perfectly matching the shade of the jersey, is laid out on the dressing table before me, beside a decorative letter 'R' copied from an early sixteenth century Polyglot Bible, a bottle of ink and my tattooist's needle.

The Act Develops

O

'Had you ever thought about working on Tom Jones having a discussion with Shirley Bassey about foundation garments?'

'Well, I hadn't.' I frowned as the comedic possibilities flooded into my mind almost instantaneously. 'But I have now.'

'Great!' Roni giggled. 'Now, what about making that Sean Connery monologue more accessible? I've had a few thoughts I'm sure you could weave into it.'

Roni picked up subtle references and allusions in my act. The truth of the matter is that she must have had to work almost as hard at identifying them as I did at slotting them into the jumble of words, songs, characters and identities. Her crumbs of praise condoned the changes she suggested. At the time, her presence went some of the way towards satisfying a newly discovered but nevertheless desperate need. She believed in me more than I believed in myself. She whole-heartedly encouraged me to stretch, develop, condense and hone my existing act. At least, she did for the first year.

I can see the outside world through the windows. I can contact the outside world via the internet and telephone. Nevertheless, this flat, apartment, living space or whatever you want to call it is my world. Even though I can feel Roni's presence, even though legally it's Roni's property, I am in control. Water, electricity and council tax (with discount for single occupancy) are paid by direct debit from Roni's bank account. Food, drink and other groceries are delivered after I've ordered them on the internet, paid for with Roni's debit card.

There were several large supermarkets offering home delivery, but I opted for a smaller company who, although slightly more expensive, put together my order from separate sources. The produce is, I believe, of better quality, but the real reason I chose them is that in their brochure they have photographs of some of their suppliers: a good old fashioned butcher, a proper baker and a delicatessen at which I can picture an apron-clad assistant weighing out my olives, my sun-dried tomatoes, my prosciutto and my parmesan cheese, which arrive in individually priced cartons as if I'd been there in the shop and asked for them myself. I can hear the bell on the door of the baker's ringing and my fresh granary rolls, my French stick and my ciabatta being put into clean crisp brown paper bags. I can imagine the butcher wielding his cleaver to separate my lamb chops, hear the disconcerting slurping noise as he pulls a pound of calf's liver from the mound under his spotlessly clean display counter, can almost see his razor sharp knife gliding effortlessly through a well-hung piece of beef fillet. It's almost as good as being there myself. Almost.

How strange it is to hanker after a visit to a butcher's shop when I'm a vegetarian.

Roni's suggestions for my act began to make sense, her ideas for new possible venues proved to be successful and – underpinning it all – the solid foundation of her support caused me to flourish. For the first time since Iris had died, I felt my life had meaning. I looked to the future with hope rather than dread; the only dread was reserved for those moments behind the curtains before I went on. But even that was reduced because I knew that what had formerly been a two-way volley between me and the audience was now a three-way exchange. I thought it was this that was allowing space for the first rays of happiness to creep into my life.

Stella barely got a look in during that time and to be quite honest it was a huge relief. She turned up from time to time to murder a song and get a laugh or two, then disappeared obediently. She knew she had met her match in Roni.

One of the biggest obstacles to happiness is the assumption that it is everyone's right to experience it. I read somewhere that the happiest place in the world – though I have no idea who expounded the time and energy on the research and by what yardstick they measured happiness – is a small island in the Pacific Ocean. I picture it as one of those places you might see on a BBC2 documentary, its inhabitants overweight and always smiling. Perhaps being born on an island – knowing that you are only ever likely to live within its bounds – reduces the urge to harbour great expectations.

My maternal grandmother used to state frequently in a confidently aloof manner that people in England were far happier back in the days 'when everyone knew their place'. I could never agree with her right up to the day she died – thinking of the miserable lives the working classes had to endure – but now I must admit that my view has changed. I can't deny that they indeed knew their places in society together with the narrow scopes their lives would inhabit, but the issue that has caused me to alter my view is that, alongside this knowledge, they had religion. It was a blind and absolute faith in the existence of a better afterlife for those who abided by its rules during their time on Earth. These people didn't need the shallow promises of the National Lottery to give them hope of a better life. With religion, providing that its demands were met, everyone was a winner.

I suppose I made a rod for my own back by letting Roni know too much too soon. Iris had known my capabilities and nurtured them, but not in order to profit from them in any way, unless companionship and a feeling of involvement could be seen as personal profit. I can't believe, looking back, that I thought Roni could be a replacement for Iris. But I *wanted* to believe that she could be. Desire for belief is its life blood.

My catalogue of life memories does include that happy courtship period when Roni virtually swept me off my feet and allowed me to think I'd found myself as a result, but I'm not sure that can actually be classed as happiness. Does a painting thought to be by an Old Master – as such holding great value – then subsequently discovered to be a clever fake still retain any residual value?

When it comes to belief, who can say where fiction ends and reality begins? Is it a necessity or a luxury? My fascination – I could almost go as far as describing it as a love affair – with the Roman Catholic church, which began when I was twelve, did not, as some have since surmised, arise from fervent beliefs either held or desired. Nor was I presented with a life-changing vision like the legendary – albeit misinterpreted – one attributed to Saint Paul on the road to Damascus. No. I became enthralled with the Roman Catholic Church because of my best friend Sarah and my dislike of horses – or, to be more precise, my complete reluctance to spend every Sunday with my family at equine events.

It was also the beginning of my realization that the members of a willing and faithful audience can be led to believe because they *want* to believe.

It was assumed by my siblings and parents that I didn't know how lucky I was to be part of a family with its own horses. I would like to think that I've never been ungrateful, but there was no getting around the fact that I didn't like them. Horses, that is, rather than my family, for whom I was unable to summon much feeling at all. Well, it's not strictly true that I didn't like horses, but I didn't like forcing them to bend to my will, so consequently they didn't obediently bend and I invariably fell off, quite often in public. The unbridled passion shared by my two older sisters for cavorting around a gymkhana ring, hammering their poor ponies into sweating submission, which was then superseded by their elation at success in two and three day events with larger animals whose increased size and strength multiplied the fruits of their persistence, not to mention days spent following the hunt (in which I couldn't even begin to think about joining), left me completely cold.

They interpreted it as fear on my part. I hardly thought this accusation warranted a reply: rather than being afraid, I was disgusted. It was the ponies and horses that were doing all the work, but my sisters – and vicariously my parents – who took all the credit. There was no point in trying to explain this to them of course. My father, a distinguished neurosurgeon who justified his arduous professional life by spending a large proportion of his income on the purchase and upkeep of horses, and my mother, an equally brilliant virologist who had been crippled in a team chasing accident at the age of thirty six when I was seven, were bewildered in their quest – not a particularly thorough one, I might add – for something for which I might show enthusiasm.

I believed, mistakenly, that they would be at least relieved if not outwardly rejoicing when I found religion. But I will return to that later.

Whatever you may have heard to the contrary, it was definitely me who suggested marriage to Roni rather than the other way around. I meant it with all my heart and soul, with all my newfound sense of self. I was sure I had found a soul mate, if not to replace Iris, to go some of the way to filling the gap left by her death. Our sex life, which I know has also been the subject of much scrutiny and speculation, also took off at my instigation rather than hers.

'No Danny!' Roni tried to slide herself out from underneath me. We were in a small hotel in Rotherham, staying in separate rooms, and my after-show elation was getting the better of me. 'You know I really like you, but please don't mistake it for something more than it is.'

'But I thought...' Words deserted me and I moved away from her as if repelled by an electric charge. It had felt so right, so natural. But I had been mistaken and now felt confused and embarrassed.

'Listen.' She sat up and reached out for me, putting an arm around my shoulders. 'Do we really want to jeopardize what we've got? We're going to go a long way together if we can manage to keep this on a platonic level.' I remained in a thwarted and confused silence, unable to believe that I had read the signs so wrongly. Unable to think of what else to do, I looked into her eyes with what must have been an expression of pleading disbelief. Whether it was caused by my naïve reaction or whether it was going to happen anyway, her features suddenly crumpled and she began to cry. Uncharacteristically pathetic sobs shuddered through her body. This sudden display of emotion was more shocking than the refusal and I couldn't have found any words to say if my life had depended on it. She eventually brought her sobbing under control and stood up, facing away from me. 'Danny, I have to tell you something.' Another agonizing silence followed as words failed me once more.

I felt sure she was about to tell me that, while she respected my talent, she found me physically repulsive. If this was the case, how could we possibly carry on working together? I faced the possibility of going back to working without her and found I didn't like it. 'The thing is, I can't have children!' She blurted out the words without turning to face me. 'Maybe that's why I'm so ambitious. I don't know. The long and the short of it is that I can't let you deprive yourself of—'

'It's *you* I want, not children!' I found words at last, stood up and wrapped my arms around her from behind. This was a side of Roni I hadn't seen before. Quite possibly, nobody had seen this side of her.

'You may say that now, Danny, but I can't risk you changing your mind.'

'Roni, I love you!'

'Really?' At that moment, she seemed so unsure of herself and childlike that my heart threatened to break.

She kept me hanging on for several more agonizing weeks until I was very nearly bursting and the night she finally gave in to my desires – in a bed and breakfast in Eastbourne – I thought I had well and truly found my destiny.

A seemingly natural progression followed to the day when I dropped down on one knee on Brighton Pier and asked her if she would do me the immense honour of becoming my wife.

It is difficult to remember now exactly what I was feeling – and I mean really feeling – back then. I do know the fact that Roni had sought me out rather than vice versa worked immeasurably in her favour. I have never gone out of my way to acquire friends and acquaintances. Roni found this strange at first, but it's part of who I am. I don't need people around me (except when I'm working of course) and I certainly have never judged myself by the social company I keep.

'We should have a dinner party to celebrate our engagement.' The sparkle in Roni's eyes wasn't remotely dimmed by the look of clear distress on my face. 'Don't worry, we'll only invite three friends.' The three friends Roni suggested inviting were – I was to come to realize – her only friends: a triumvirate I was later to think of as The Friends.

She had moved into my little Battersea flat the week before and my fears and reservations about co-habitation had been allayed. Delicious warm waves of affection wafted through me as we snuggled together in bed at the end of each long day. I began to wonder how I had managed on my own for all those years. I wanted her. I needed her. God help me, I loved her. The joys of reaching out in the early hours of the morning to find her warm sleeping body beside me outweighed by far the anticipated loss of privacy and space for quiet reflection. 'Which of us is going to cook?' I felt fear welling up inside me. Entertaining strangers in my home – our home – seemed to me to be a recipe for disaster.

'We'll get food brought in.' Roni dismissed my fears with the wave of a hand. 'We can afford it now.' It was true that we were beginning to earn a reasonable living from our joint efforts and, now Roni had moved in with me, we only had one monthly rent payment between us. She was already talking about putting the money we were saving towards financing a tour – further evidence of her unswerving faith in my abilities. 'Next Wednesday it is then. You don't need to worry about anything. Just be yourself.'

As the day of the dinner party loomed closer, I felt my anxiety levels rising. Of course, I had plenty to distract me with the daily implementation of the changes and improvements to my act, but all the time the nagging fears that I would not be able to function in a social setting and would let Roni down in front of her friends kept surfacing.

A possible plan of action revealed itself to me when we were out walking a few days later. The morning had been a distressing one because I had come into the living room to find the door of the doves' cage wide open, the only sign of its former inhabitants being a white feather caught on the latch of the open window. Roni had tried to commiserate with me.

'They'll be happier flying free,' she said kindly, 'and it's not as if you need the dove pan in your act any more.'

'But they'll be lost out in the world.' I thought of Faith, Hope and Charity – as I had named my delicate little white birds – flying about looking for a way back to their cage.

'Remember that they chose to fly away,' she said, tilting her head to one side with a sympathetic expression on her face, 'but we'll leave the window open for them in case they come back. Now let's go out for a walk to cheer ourselves up.' So we ventured out on foot to Lavender Hill. I couldn't help myself looking up at the sky to see if I could catch a glimpse of white feathers flashing by. Needless to say, I didn't. Then, fortunately, my attention was drawn to the window of a small antique shop.

'Look, I think they're late Spode.' I pointed at some exquisite blue and white plates. 'Aren't they beautiful?'

'Let's buy them!' Roni grasped my upper arm excitedly. 'They'll be just right for Wednesday.' She was right. They would sit perfectly on the dining table I had made from a circular piece of glass balanced on a large Grecian style urn I'd discovered in a Bermondsey reclamation yard. It would help create the illusion that we held dinner parties as frequently as I changed my guise. And that was what it was all about, wasn't it, creating an illusion?

'And they'll think we've been slaving over a hot stove for hours poring over our grandmothers' recipes, when really the food's just been delivered!' For the first time, I felt a flicker of eager anticipation. I suddenly began to understand why people had dinner parties. I felt included.

I think this might be the right time to confirm that, even though it might be memory playing its fitful tricks again, my ability to control Stella during that period was definitely down to a new inner strength I had found thanks to Roni. On the other hand, my new character might have been responsible, although I'm almost sure that he didn't come into being until the day of the dinner party.

'So what on earth are we going to call you?' Ellie Franklin, self-acclaimed agent to and occasional bedfellow of some of the most successful sports personalities of the era raised her glass (not the first of the evening) of alarmingly expensive red wine and addressed me raucously in an accent that advertised privilege and inborn self-confidence. 'You can't go on calling yourself the fucking *Chameleon* for God's sake!'

'I know!' Now it was the turn of Neil Ashcroft, someone who would still to this day be quite perturbed that you didn't immediately recognize his name. He produced television adverts – and lots of them – mostly starring Ellie's clients. 'When we heard our Roni had gone and got herself engaged to some *impersonator*,' he almost spat the word out, 'we weren't quite ready for the bundle of fun you've proved yourself to be.'

'More than that, my darlings, he's going to be a *huge* star!' Rex Avalon, self-styled PR guru, of whom I know you *will* have heard but who was then still relatively unknown, gushed. 'He needs a big name. Something like Eastwood. How does that sound? Danny Eastwood?'

'I thought Redgrave.' Roni was standing behind my chair massaging, or rather fondling, my shoulders. I could see our reflections in the large gilt-framed mirror on the wall opposite the dining table. She looked happy and proud in a well-fitting wrap-around dress made of soft crepe in a rich burgundy that accentuated her well-toned curves. A heavy white metal chain at her throat, coupled with a smaller version on her right wrist, hinted at the strength behind the apparent tenderness of her appearance. I looked, I thought, strangely confident in front of her. This was how I appeared to my audiences, but this was the first time I had entertained one in my own home. 'Danny Redgrave has a real ring to it.' I could tell that our dinner party had exceeded Roni's wildest expectations and was pleased that I hadn't let her down.

'No no no... Douglas!' Ellie flicked a white silk scarf, which was the only soft aspect to the appearance she presented, back over her right shoulder to conceal an ample but unwelcoming cleavage. 'Danny Douglas!'

The conversations – or monologues as they quite often were – of these friends of Roni's came from a very self-satisfied stance I found alien and nauseating. They were their own audience, but had given me their stamp of approval. Was I meant to feel honoured? Thanks to the armour provided by my new character, I was able to stomach their approval and conceal the fact that I was tiring of their apparent need to find the reasons and roots for everything. Why couldn't something be accepted for what it was?

'Ride from the seat of your pants!' my mother used to shout from her wheelchair. 'Don't think about it, just do it!'

I spoke up and told them that, despite their helpful suggestions, my new working name was to be Devereux. Danny Devereux. I didn't tell them why, because I didn't feel the need. *I* knew why and that was all that mattered. The long and the short of it was that my new character, which was to become the new 'me', was willed into being by imagining what Iris would have said or done in any given situation: a simple premise that was going to have far-reaching consequences.

Now, more than ten years later, the same burgundy crepe dress Roni wore that night is hanging on the wardrobe door behind me as I begin my three hour preparation. I can see its reflection as I lean forward to get the full benefit of the lights around the mirror to achieve the effect I am looking for with my make-up. A white metal necklace and bracelet sit on the dressing table glinting in the light as if in anticipation of the part they are about to play in the transformation. The newly sterilized electric needle is ready beside them.

You could be forgiven for asking if I think I am playing God in this plan that I have hatched. Maybe I am. Don't we all like to feel that we are in charge of our destinies? No doubt it would be easier to surrender to life's consequences and accept the role of victim, although I can't imagine doing that and retaining any quality of life.

When the body of tonight's Night Delivery is pulled from the river, he will probably be known prior to formal identification simply as 'O'.

The Wedding

N

'You may now kiss the bride.' The registrar smiled kindly as I obeyed her suggestion and eagerly embraced Roni. Our lips met and, in that moment, I suddenly knew why it is said that your wedding day is the best day of your life. Ellie and Rex – our witnesses in the simple civil ceremony at Chelsea Register Office – clapped their hands together and cheered behind us. Neil followed suit, but noticeably less enthusiastically, despite his assurances that he hadn't been in the least offended at not being asked to be a witness.

My vows were spoken from the heart on that day and I truly felt that we would be together forever: soul mates first and partners in business second. I didn't mind that the surviving members of my family were either unable or indisposed to attend. The truth of the matter was that my father had descended into an incoherently alcoholic stupor that never seemed to abate, his brilliant and analytical mind unable to cope with the facts that he had ceased to be useful and that my mother was no longer by his side. My elder sister had married an Australian farmer and emigrated years earlier. The younger one was married to a born-again-Christian architect and lived in Coventry, probably as oblivious to the irony of her husband's religious fervour (when the family had been so horrified at my Catholic 'phase') as she was to the fabled obscurity of the city in which she was destined to spend the rest of her life. I didn't need them any more. I hadn't, in fact, needed them for years. Any sense of belonging to or being needed by my family, which may have at one time existed, had disappeared years earlier. I had learned, by necessity, to exist without them.

Now, however, I felt that I was living rather than just existing because Roni had brought new meaning to my life and made me realize what I had been missing in my solitude. 'We don't need family,' Roni said as she squeezed my hand, 'we've got each other now.' I took this as meaning that she too – after years spent alone in the world following her mother's death – felt that we were capable of taking on the world now that we were together. Our mutual absence of family on whom to rely for emotional support gave us the incentive and desire to allow this partnership we had forged to grow into something unyielding and palpable. Not for us the rules laid down for lesser mortals. We didn't need to toe a line drawn by a pre-defined moral code. Our relationship was ours and ours alone. On that day, to coin a phrase, it truly felt as if the world was our oyster.

When my mother had her accident, my father was, I now realize, completely unable to cope. More than that, he was apparently unable – or unwilling – to accept the fact that his wife and soul mate wouldn't make the full recovery he categorically knew as a medical man was impossible. My sisters stayed at home to look after him on the infrequent and irregular occasions he came back from the hospitals (the ones in which he performed his skilful mobility-saving operations and the one in which my immobile mother was ensconced) and I was sent to stay with my maternal grandmother in Surrey.

Even at the tender age of seven, without knowing the word itself, I knew that Grandma was an anachronism. Born into a family which had made its money in household furniture at the turn of the century, she had married the son of a local landowner for social rather than romantic reasons, grew in time to love him (or so she once began to tell me in a moment of uncharacteristic sentimental reflection) and was almost forty when my mother – their only child – was born just before the war. She was widowed less than two years later. I can see now that her slightly odd behaviour was a symptom of the survival system she had devised.

For her, life had a script which needed to be followed rigidly. The slightest deviation from it would be interpreted as showing signs of moral weakness. In her fondly remembered and much-lamented world, everyone was expected to know their role and be aware of the penalty for daring to get 'above themselves'. She made no secret of the fact that she held the war responsible for eroding this stratification of purpose. The national sense of post-war freedom from the terrible threat of a German invasion was not for her. The class system had been levelled out and her way of life seriously jeopardized.

'I have a special treat lined up for us today, Daniel,' she said to me one morning as we sat eating a breakfast of poached eggs on toast at the polished mahogany table in the breakfast room.

'Every day here is a treat, Grandma.' Even at that tender age, I could detect that she was finding my presence awkward and wanted to put her at her ease. Through the crinkled Georgian glass of the floor-to-ceiling French windows, I could see the clean sweep of the newly-mown lawn, beyond which the rear of a row of suburban semi-detached villas was clearly visible. The land they were built on had belonged to my grandfather and his father before him. I knew these houses were inhabited by 'factory foremen, architects and bank managers', although I wasn't at all sure why this was a bad thing, only that it must be because of the tone of voice she employed for stating the fact. I now realize that the sale of the land had enabled her to remain living in the family house. For her, having to leave this final stronghold of her position in life would have spelt the end of her existence being worthwhile.

I can vividly remember my parents discussing the hold my grandmother had tried to exert over them when they were first married. They used to laugh about her and compliment each other on the combined independence they had achieved for themselves and their children entirely though their own efforts. But that was before my mother's accident.

'Would you like to know what the treat is?' I was struggling to finish my eggs – worried as I always was when I saw the orange yolk flowing over my toast that I was depriving a never-to-be-born chick of its life – so she didn't wait for my answer. 'I have acquired a film for us to watch.'

The large old television set kept in a room off the kitchen (definitely not in the drawing room that was reserved for the purpose of receiving her exceedingly infrequent visitors) was something my grandmother used almost exclusively for watching the news, royal weddings and – most recently – the Queen's silver jubilee celebrations. But a few days earlier she had, in an uncharacteristic flash of extravagance, invested in a Betamax video machine. Looking back, I think she must have been thinking of me when she bought it – evidence, perhaps, that the stern exterior with which she faced the world did after all conceal an inner softness that was capable of giving love.

A woman in her seventies faced suddenly and unexpectedly with the task of caring for a young and impressionable child, she must have been concerned and frightened. I can imagine her struggling to find the expected and correct way to proceed in these unforeseen circumstances.

I remember distinctly that later that day, as we sat side by side on the uncomfortable sofa watching 'Mrs Miniver', she actually put her arm around me and pulled me towards her. 'You're my second chance to get things right,' she said quietly. I really didn't know at the time what she meant, so why have I remembered her words for all these years?

Did she know that my mother would be changed beyond recognition when she eventually came out of hospital? Had she, with the wisdom of age, realized that my life would never be the same again in the same way that hers hadn't been since the war? I moved closer to her as Greer Garson watched anxiously for her husband to return from Dunkirk having single-handedly dealt with a German officer in her kitchen. My young heart sank as I felt her draw away. She had obviously extended her limits as far as she was able. I drew back to my side of the sofa and lost myself once again in the perfectly-spoken dialogue accompanying the actions on the screen.

Our wedding reception took place in a small restaurant off the King's Road – somewhere Roni and I had discovered in the early days of her being my manager – and the gay couple who ran it had been delighted when we decided to use it as a venue for our celebration. Our budget was obviously limited, but they prepared delightful canapés and decorated the place with swathes of white muslin and huge arrangements of white flowers. The only extravagance was real champagne. I knew Iris would have approved. 'Never scrimp on the bubbles or they'll come back to haunt you,' she had cackled delightedly once as we shared a vintage bottle she had sent me out to purchase at her expense to celebrate one of my birthdays. The sadness I always felt at being reminded that she was no longer living was tinged with happiness that she would have given her blessing to this marriage. I raised my glass to Roni and smiled. Then the happiness suddenly threatened to evaporate as Ellie Franklin appeared behind Roni with an all too familiar look of pitying superiority on her face.

'Cheers!' Her cut glass accent sliced through the air as she raised her well-charged glass with one hand and flicked the signature silk scarf over her shoulder with the other. 'I really wish you'd allowed me to help you afford somewhere more *suitable* for your reception.'

Roni didn't say anything in reply. She didn't need to. The look on her face said it all. She was hurt, as only I knew how she could be. At the time it nearly broke my heart to see her bravely pretend that Ellie's words hadn't hit home. Looking back with the obvious benefit of hindsight, although of course it might be my memory playing its fickle tricks again, I realize that it was more likely that she was genuinely upset that we weren't celebrating somewhere more chic and upmarket. At the time, though, I believed that she was happy with our celebration because I wanted to believe it.

'Who says you can't have fun on a shoestring?' I put my arm around Roni's shoulders, feeling her tense with the effort to ignore Ellie's words. Or that's what I thought was making her tense. Perhaps she was wondering whether she had made the right move. Was she questioning the power of her steely resolve to make of me the success she had envisaged? Back then, I was blissfully unaware of the extent of the machinations of the mind of Veronica Bedford.

I truly think that our wedding reception was the last time I was myself rather than 'myself' in public.

My grandmother had a parrot she referred to as 'The Duke'. He was an African Grey of indeterminate age and must have been caught in the wild many years earlier. He had apparently been a wedding present from a titled relation. Her only company for much of the time until I encroached on her existence, she must have felt a great affinity with him; they were both survivors adrift in an alien world. She showed him affection when he obeyed her, which is another reason I know she had a well-hidden tender aspect to her character. I was fascinated with the way he would obediently lift a claw to 'shake hands' in order to be rewarded with a peanut, but more enamoured with his ability to mimic short phrases (parts of the National Anthem and the Lord's Prayer being present in his repertoire).

Grandma would try to conceal her delight at his abilities, but I knew his antics pleased her. I wanted to please her too, to see her forced to surrender a smile on my account.

Following the wedding, I was expecting a level of domestic calm to descend on our home life. After all, we had made a commitment to each other, pledging mutual support and love to enhance our lives together. Work was obviously important, but I saw it as a means to an end: we were fortunate to have found each other and be able to work together. Our respective talents and abilities came together to form the whole that was our working relationship. Roni had taken from me the burden of having to push and sell myself and I wanted to do something in return, something to make her work more pleasurable.

One day when she was out meeting with a club promoter to discuss a series of bookings, I had stayed at home to 'revise'. This was a process that came as second nature to me now – going through the newspapers, watching the news on television and listening to the radio. I merely absorbed as much current information as I could to top up the pool from which I could draw during my act. I have already said that it was impossible to rehearse what I did in front of the public, but I needed to have the raw material at my disposal. While I was doing it, I was able to eat, drink tea and sometimes read the biographies of eminent film stars, authors and politicians that have always fascinated me so. I have always been able to concentrate on several things at once and didn't really think it was a particular talent until Roni drew attention to the fact one day in a restaurant, while we were deep in conversation, that I was also able to quietly listen to the hushed argument of a couple at the next table.

This particular day, it suddenly occurred to me that the surface of Roni's desk was devoid of anything remotely personal. It was a dark Victorian Neo-Gothic piece decorated with carved lion's heads I had picked up in a junk shop on the Roman Road several years earlier. It had a battered maroon inlaid leather top and drawers down each side in which she kept her carefully-filed records of gigs, payments and bank statements. Apart from the telephone and a large desk diary, its surface was bare. Clean, because I polished it every day, but bare. Since she spent so long sitting at it, I thought I would add a few touches to brighten it up. The News Quiz was playing on the radio as I busied myself arranging a small framed photo of us on our wedding day, a Christmas cactus that had recently burst into impressive bloom, which I placed in a Chinese bowl that had been my grandmother's, and a selection of books from around the flat. As I did it, I felt guilty that I hadn't thought of it sooner. When she spent so long persisting with her telephone enquiries and doggedly filling up the diary with bookings, the least I could do would be to make her work space a little more pleasant. We were, after all, in this together. We were a team.

I heard Roni's key in the door just as I had settled down with three of the daily newspapers and a fresh pot of Earl Grey tea in front of me. I jumped up and went to the kitchen to get her a cup. As I came back into the living room, she was wordlessly removing my additions to her desk and didn't even look up as I placed the cup on the coffee table and began to pour. 'How did the meeting go?' I tried to keep the disappointment out of my voice, for it was genuine disappointment that I was feeling.

'I haven't got time for all this nonsense.' The wedding photograph went face-down on the mantelpiece as she said it. 'You were meant to be working, not pissing around with pot plants!'

I didn't tell her that I *had* been working, that I had been trying to make things better for her, that our work didn't have to be separate from our home life. I didn't tell her, because I assumed she was feeling stressed from having to deal with the promoters. I actually felt sorry for her. I loved her. And I was *in* love with her.

If I had realized back then where this was all going to lead, I can't say with any honesty what I would have done about it. But that isn't what this memoir is about. I am sitting here in this showpiece apartment, that doesn't even belong to me any more, putting all my energy into purely recording the facts. You may ask why I feel the need to do so and that is another question I can't really answer beyond saying that I have a desire to see the events – and emotions – in written form. It's not satisfaction I'm seeking. I have a sneaking suspicion that it is because I am testing my ability to tell the truth.

Today there is a further distraction from this already difficult task. Even though it is a bright sunny day outside, I have had to make sure that all the curtains and blinds are firmly closed because the window cleaner, who is paid from Roni's account with a monthly direct debit, is at work outside. I can hear him whistling happily as he goes about his business –

just another job in another busy working week, just another week in another working year during which he will have earned his living and justified his existence. The tune he's chosen is 'There's No Business Like Show Business', which seems to be a strange choice for a window cleaner and plunges me into memories of Ethel Merman fighting for stage space with Stella in the Early Days.

I think it was largely a mock battle as they seemed to like each other: Ethel's entire stage presence revolved around her massive singing voice, no more, no less, while Stella had everything *except* a singing voice and made a seemingly endless point of it with her extensive repertoire of songs that invariably brought the house down. The first number she ever sang on stage was 'Living Doll', which had to be heard – and seen – to be believed. She had a knack and ability to growl her way through a number, put in a bit of hip gyration and tit shaking and make it hilarious with the minimum of apparent effort. Secure in her knowledge and possession of this ability, Stella didn't feel compromised or threatened by Ethel's presence in the act. Any bitchery between them was light hearted and, anyway, Ethel used to just do a song and disappear. You always knew where you were with Ethel Merman.

'There's No Business Like Show Business.' The window cleaner's still belting it out. Does he see his work as a performance, I wonder? I suppose there are similarities: when he does his job well, it's easy not to notice, but if he does his job badly, it's impossible to overlook the mistakes – streaks and smears jump out at you like wrong notes and backfiring jokes.

I wonder what he'd think if he knew I was in here, concealed from his view by nothing more than a few layers of chiffon. He would be onto a hot story – yet another chance for the paparazzi to get their money's worth out of me. I can imagine any number of headlines – 'Disgraced Star In Exile in Riverside Apartment' being one of them. The story would net him a lot more than the seventy pounds a month he receives for cleaning Roni's windows. Any of the daily papers would pay good money to learn that I'm here, rather than in hiding in the Caribbean, which is where I am according to the last report I leaked. I suppose I should be flattered that anyone is still interested, but that would rely on me having cared in the first place.

The cheery window cleaner is lucky that he doesn't know I'm here; lucky that he doesn't know and therefore isn't tempted.

But I must force myself back to the task I have set for myself and record the facts as honestly as I can. The two years following our wedding passed remarkably quickly. A century and a millennium ended. Another century and another millennium began, although I'm not sure I ever shared Roni's high expectations of it. A practically non-stop succession of gigs and appearances left little time for reflection on the direction in which my career (for it had now become a 'career' rather than just an occupation) was going.

It may seem as if I'm dismissive of my part in the process, but I can assure you that nothing could be further from the truth. I pursued our goal obsessively – the advantage of which was that I didn't, as I have just said, have time for private deliberation on what I was doing. But now I'm contradicting myself, because how could it be an advantage? I think I am trying to say that it made life easier. There is absolutely no doubt in my mind that I was obsessed.

My obsession was pleasing Roni.

I really don't think I can have grasped the full extent of Roni's drive and determination. I see now that, in her mind, there was never any doubt that this was all going to lead somewhere. She had an unerring ability to focus on goals and give meaning to the daily struggle in which we were engaged. I, on the other hand, was so accustomed to life being a struggle that I was content – or as close to the state as was possible for me to be – that I was no longer alone, that I had an ally both in my precarious profession and in my private life. Unlike Roni, I wasn't counting the days as they passed, wondering how long it would be before a breakthrough came, because I didn't feel that we needed one. I did often count the hours until the day was over, looking forward to the precious minutes we shared before we went to bed – a welcome and private time when we would drink tea and unwind from the strains of the day, often communicating without speaking. I wasn't seized with a desperate need for success, since I thought I'd found it in this rare and beautiful partnership we had created.

The more I think about it, the more I am tempted to believe that I really was content in those days, a contentment derived not inconsiderably from the fact that I had never anticipated or expected such a sensation to permeate my being.

'Goodbye Mr Chips' was one of the films that followed 'Mrs Miniver' and I became, in the privacy of my bedroom at Grandma's, an expert mimic of Greer Garson's clipped tones. Some inner reserve thankfully kept me from showing my grandmother what I could do. While the intention must have been there, particularly when I watched her fussing delightedly around her parrot, I can only imagine in retrospect what her reaction would have been.

I can't really define the point at which each individual impression ceased to be part of my act, where each of my characters stopped appearing, where I found myself spending an hour and a half – sometimes more – on stage just being Danny Devereux. This is not to say that this new character of mine was without conflict. I didn't like him a great deal, but could see that the audiences did. Coupled with that, there were a lot of possible gigs coming our way – as stand-up comedy took an increasing hold on the nation – where it would have been not only inappropriate but also impossible to incorporate costume changes and props into the act.

There were times when I yearned to be able to revert to some of my old fail-safe material, to become

Marlene Dietrich again, to resurrect the Duke of Edinburgh doing a cockney music hall number or make the crowd beg for more Dusty Springfield, but Roni urged me on and saw me through. She treated me as if I needed to rid myself of these old habits. In her eyes, I was like a heroin addict who needed to get through one day at a time without reverting to harmful behaviour.

I have to admit that, when it came to Stella, I agreed with her.

'Trust me, Danny,' she would say, letting a hint of tenderness creep into her voice, bringing with it the inference that she was offended that I might possibly *not* trust her. 'This talent you have is a gift and you mustn't waste it.'

Her words of encouragement were all I had to keep me from becoming completely paralysed with fear when I was waiting to go on stage. The smaller the venue, the worse the trepidation that gripped my insides. In a large venue, once the curtains swished back, it was virtually impossible to see individual faces in the audience. They became a single entity, a force with which I was going into combat. In a small place like the new breed of comedy clubs, it was a different story entirely. I could actually see individual faces in the crowd. They belonged to real people, each with his or her own individual personality, thoughts and feelings. Each of them had made the conscious decision to come and see me perform. Each of them expected to be entertained – and entertained by me alone.

'Just be yourself,' Roni said.

What is wrong with what Roni did? I am asking myself as much as I am asking you. Was it the lack of honesty? Was it the pretence at sincerity? Of course not. The reason I feel that Roni deserves what is coming to her is simple: she allowed me to laugh, to feel secure and even to feel loved. And what, I can almost hear you asking, is wrong with that?

The answer is simple.

If she hadn't, I would never have known what it felt like. But I would have survived without it.

Love. What is it? I thought I knew what it was back then. I wanted to please Roni – or wanted to see the results of her being pleased. A favourable response from her induced a warm tide to flood through my body – a physical sensation on which I became reliant. One addiction had given way to another.

And that love, or what I took to be love, was made stronger by the fact that I had to fight for it. Not only because I had to meet Roni's considerable demands, but because I also had to fight for her attention. The Friends seemed to be a constant presence, always giving their opinions. Roni was continually looking to them for their seal of approval. It grieved me to see her trying to show them that her chosen career – managing me – was as good as their respective professions. I fervently wanted her to be able to show them that she was better than them.

'The television camera's more of a test than you could ever know.' Ellie Franklin had a supercilious sneer on her face. 'There's no way Danny's ready for it.' Roni had merely dared to mention that one of Ellie's clients, a footballer who was fast becoming a media star in his own right following a series of adverts for designer underwear and a stint as host on a quiz show, was surprisingly dull when you met him in the flesh.

'I wasn't comparing him with Danny.' Roni put her arm around me.

'Good!' Ellie's determined expression suddenly gave way to the girlie laugh that never fooled me. But I didn't like the way she was always trying to belittle Roni. My Roni.

More than once, the presence of Ellie in the audience made me try harder, caused me to push myself beyond the limits my former achievements had set for me. I didn't want her to be able to look at Roni knowingly. It cut me to the quick when she put her down with that haughty laugh and a razor sharp flick of a flimsy silk scarf.

It must have been at this time, unbeknown to me, that Rex and Roni were beginning to cook up a story between them which, when it hit the news, was useful, well-timed and, above all, believable. But that is what Rex has become famous for, after all. The extremely mediocre actress caught having an affair with a prominent and very married MP – the object of his first big success – is still living off the proceeds of the consequent career he made for her. But I digress. All the time that I was innocently besotted with my wife and pouring all of my affection for her into trying to make her proud of me, I can now see that she was plotting ahead to the next big career move. And part of that career move was the story about my past she was concocting with Rex.

I am watching some video footage of me performing at The Comedy Café in Rivington Street shot by Neil Ashcroft. Roni insisted we had everything on tape so that we could dissect what worked and what didn't. The videos, along with my notes, now fill the shelves in the study. Today, for the first time in years, I felt the need to watch a piece of my past. The reason I chose this particular show is that it came right before the train of events that led up to my first television appearance. I look at myself strutting on that small stage to all intents and purposes completely confident in myself – or 'myself'. I'm picking items at random from the news, taking comments hurled from the audience and turning them into something tangible, ironic and above all funny. I can see it as the audience saw it at the time. I can see how Rex Avalon saw it. I can see how Ellie Franklin saw it. I can see how Roni saw it. But I can't for the life of me remember how I actually felt inside.

Can we ever truly remember feelings?

When I say that I don't really know when I first discovered my talent for mimicry, I mean it in the same way as not being able to remember learning to speak, but I can definitely pinpoint the first time I used my talent to my advantage. It was in the changing rooms after a particularly unpleasant game of rugby (a game of which I have never been able to either see the point or grasp the rules). For reasons best known only to them, two of the school's current bullies had decided it was my turn to be chased around the showers with a bucket of cold water. This was actually nothing out of the ordinary, since my schooldays were a long series of traumatic experiences. I suppose I survived them because I imagined all my fellow pupils were going through the same agonies, putting on a brave face and generally doing what was necessary to get through one day at a time. In actual fact, I feel sorry for children nowadays who are brought up to believe it is their right to be happy. If I had been born later, I have no doubt about the fact that I would have been a candidate for constant counselling. Perhaps I would have been happier as a result.

Perhaps not.

My survival technique at school involved, in a manner that at the time seemed perfectly normal to me, imagining what people like Mae West, John Wayne, Gloria Swanson or even Margaret Thatcher would do or say in a particular situation. If I was analysing my childhood, I would say that my fascination with these characters went some of the way towards filling the void left by the absence of love from my mother after her accident, but I'm not analysing it. Or maybe I am and pointedly denying the fact, which is – in itself – fodder for analysis. Either way, my sudden loud impression of the games master admonishing my two burly tormentors stopped them in their tracks, giving me the time to escape. When it became clear to the assembled company that I had got the better of them, not to mention how I'd done it, it induced an appreciative round of applause. It was to become the first of many.

So, one minute I was sitting in the small dressing room upstairs at the Comedy Café gathering my thoughts and wondering what Roni was up to (for I wasn't completely oblivious to what was going on around me), the next Roni swept in with Ellie and a man with spiky hair, horn-rimmed spectacles, tweed jacket and bright red training shoes. He thrust his hand towards me and introduced himself as Bing Alexander. A little taken aback by his strange name, I couldn't help wondering if he had been christened with it and that, if he had, what on earth had possessed his parents to look down at their little baby and decide to name it 'Bing'. Mind you, the same thing goes through my mind when I encounter people called 'Gladys', 'Reginald' or 'Ethel'. The commotion caused by three of them talking at once brought me out of my reverie and back to the present.

'The thing is,' Bing was saying with great animation, 'we haven't got any time to—'

'I know!' Roni shouted, 'but don't expect us to just drop everything—'

'For fuck's sake!' Ellie slammed her fist down on the dressing table, knocking over a styrofoam cup of cold coffee. 'This is a chance in a—'

'I'm over a barrel here!' Bing shouted.

'But we don't know what—' Roni waved her arm in the air and inadvertently poked Ellie in the eye.

'Ow!' Ellie glared at Roni with pure hatred in her eyes, or at least the eye that hadn't been poked. I knew I had to do something and do it fast. For some unaccountable reason, Muhammed Ali put words in my mouth as I drew myself up to my full height to deliver them.

"*Float like a butterfly. Sting like a bee. Your hands can't hit what your eyes can't see!*"

I didn't mean them to come out quite as loudly as they did, but they had the desired effect. Ellie fell silent, Roni turned away from Ellie and looked at me in surprise and Bing – who it later transpired was an avid Ali fan – looked delighted and roared with laughter. 'That's good enough for me. He's got the job! Now let's get to the bloody studio now!'

What I found out a little later, while being whisked to the television studios on the South Bank, was that Ellie's football player client who was currently the host of a sports quiz entitled 'A Game of Two Halves' had been struck down with a mystery illness. The show was going out live that evening and another host had to be found in record time.

There is a deep blue power suit and cream silk blouse hanging on the wardrobe door behind me. It pre-dates me in Roni's life, having been bought at the time when she was still battling against the odds to carve a career for herself in musical theatre. She must have been the only musical actress to turn up to auditions dressed like a lawyer. Her point and aim was to set herself apart from the rest, but it wasn't enough. *She* wasn't enough. And that was what she couldn't bear – the cold, hard fact that she hadn't got what it took. But bitterness, resentment and drive she had in increasing abundance. And to give credit where it is due, she was no stranger to hard work. She once told me that she remembered – and I mean vividly remembered – every single casting and audition right down to the most minute detail.

I've chosen make-up from that period, or at least evoking it: soft pearlized foundation with pastel blusher and peach lipstick – a soft look to contrast with the business-like suit. There was always method to Roni's actions.

I carefully copied tonight's letter – 'N' – from the Good News Bible and it now sits on the desk in front of me with the bottle of ink and needle. Every night the task is getting easier. At least it's getting physically easier. Mentally, it can be more than a little draining. Last night's Delivery wanted to tell me his reasons and motivation. For God's sake! Did he think it was a bloody audition?

I don't know whether to put it down to the extremely frantic nature of that evening, blame it on the lack of opportunity for me to refuse to do it or simply attribute it to the enormous rush of adrenalin surging through my veins, but I can hardly remember anything of the run-up to that first television appearance once we'd left the comedy club. I do know that it has since been said that it was that last-minute opportunity that assured my career and paved the way for the great things that were to come. While this is undoubtedly true, what really irritates me is the intimation that, from that point on, it was all plain sailing. Nothing – and I can't emphasize the point clearly enough – could be further from the truth. It was very much the beginning. In pulling off the last-minute appearance, I had metaphorically scaled a mountain, only to find at its peak that it was the smallest of a whole range formerly hidden behind the first.

There is concrete evidence (if the published word can be described as concrete or taken as evidence) that the viewers loved my performance, with particular mention of the manner in which I handled the sports celebrities 'as if they were ordinary people'. I find this quote amusing because it assumes that I was cleverly daring to pretend not to recognize their status, when in reality I (and 'I') had absolutely no idea who any of them were before I hurriedly read the programme notes. So, in that respect at least, I *was* being myself.

There is no doubt that my performance that night served as an acknowledgement that Roni's creation (otherwise known as the new 'me') was a marketable commodity.

I'm in my bedroom – my perfectly designed, perfectly clean, eclectically religious purple, black and white hermitage. Through the windows I can see the river – or at least the light from the moon and buildings around reflecting off the slightly rippling surface of the water; it is calm tonight. I have been ready for only a few minutes, having now perfected this nightly routine, and am preparing to stand before the closed curtains for precisely thirty seconds after the intercom goes and my Night Delivery is on his way in. Those thirty seconds will pass before I part the curtains, make an entrance on the gangway and another young man succumbs to the re-created charms of Veronica Bedford.

The Tour

I

'The timing is perfect, Rex.' Roni was talking excitedly on the phone as I wandered into the kitchen the next morning. My sleep had been deep but troubled. I remember – or think I remember – a particularly disturbing dream in which Roni was dragging me through a town in a large brightly-coloured cage on wheels. 'Release the story now!'

'What story?' I asked. She put her finger to her lips to silence me before continuing.

'A magazine feature would be perfect, but a few little newspaper stories would be just as good.' She smiled to herself as I watched her, my perplexity mounting. 'He's about to hit the big time if we handle it right. Thank God we had the story ready.' I touched her arm gently and looked at her questioningly, but she brushed my hand away. 'Okay. Leak it if you think that's best. Yes, I'm sure you're right!' She nodded frantically into the receiver as if he could see her. 'Of course I trust you! It's in your hands Rex. Just let me know how it's going. Speak to you later.' She ended the call looking elated.

'What's going on?' I felt uneasy.

'Nothing for you to worry about, my darling.' She walked through to the living room and sat at her clear desk. 'Just rest assured that I'm doing what a good manager does. Any coffee going?'

I failed to make any more sense of the situation that morning, but by early afternoon I had been offered guest appearances on no less than three chat shows. 'It's started, Danny!' Roni kissed me exuberantly on the lips. 'Didn't I tell you I could do it?' The first chat show was that evening and, because I didn't have a booking that night, she had accepted it without hesitation.

'But what will they want to talk about?' I wasn't naïve enough to think that the information she was keeping from me wasn't important.

'You were brilliant last night!' She kissed me again. 'That's what they'll want to talk about. Now make sure you're well rested. We have to be there at five.' I still hadn't fully recovered from the pressure of the live show the night before, so – realizing she wasn't going to tell me anything else – went to lie down for a couple of hours, wondering how the chat show interview would work, how the presenters would be in real life. I had seen them in action: a fifty-something old-time all-rounder with a burnished copper tan and his glamorous young female co-presenter. On the surface, they formed a picture of smiles, perfect white teeth and healthy skin, which made it difficult to believe the rumours that they hated each other off-screen and were famously unforgiving to difficult guests.

As I dozed fitfully, I distinctly remember feeling that this development signalled the end of a way of life rather than a beginning.

I was right.

I truly believe that you only ever really miss things when you categorically can't have them, like Tetley tea or Marmite when you've been abroad for a long time, regardless of whether or not you would want them when you are at home and they are in plentiful and easily accessible supply. This morning I am sitting on a wicker chair, the pale grey muslin curtains edged with orange and gold Indian brocade slightly parted, a bone china cup of Earl Grey tea with a slice of lemon in front of me on a wicker side table. I am gazing out across the river in the direction of Fortnum and Mason's, where the tea came from. I can't see it from here of course, but I know where it is and I can picture it in my mind's eye. I can picture the box of Earl Grey on the shelf amongst the Lapsang Souchong and the English Breakfast tea. I can envisage myself picking it up, taking it to the frock-coated cashier and paying for it. I can imagine, with the eau de nil carrier bag bearing the impressive crest in my hand, strolling easily down Piccadilly without a care in the world.

I yearn for it because it has been impossible for years. Before, it was impossible because I was a celebrity. Now, it's impossible because I never leave this apartment.

Later that day, as I was waiting with Roni in the green room minutes before the start of the show, a slim confident-looking girl wearing torn jeans and a peculiarly revealing top (considering she clearly didn't have much to reveal) approached us with a clipboard.

'Gerry and Lil are really laid back,' she squawked loudly, 'but I just need to run through the answers you're going to give to the questions we've prepared.' Roni hurriedly jumped up to intercept her and spoke quietly, gesticulating emphatically, and my anxiety levels shot up alarmingly. Whatever was going on, I needed to know about it and know right then that instant. The girl walked away, looking nervously over her shoulder at me. Roni came back and sat beside me, but her attempts to pretend I had nothing to worry about didn't fool me.

'Please tell me what's going on.' I felt even more nervous than I normally did before a show; yet another boundary of possibility had been expanded.

'We're making you into a star, that's what's going on.' This embodiment of smug satisfaction and blatant mystery wasn't the Roni I knew and loved. She was scaring me.

'What do you mean "we"?' It wasn't the question foremost in my mind, but I was beginning to lose my focus. I could feel panic rising in my chest. I suddenly realized I needed to vomit and leapt up from my seat and looked about wildly for the nearest lavatory.

'Where are you going?' Roni jumped up and was at my side in an instant. I swear she looked frightened. In retrospect, I can see that she thought I was about to make a run for it. At the time, all I could think about was my imminent need to vomit and the whereabouts of a lavatory in which to do it. My eyes frantically scanned for and found one and I darted into it, Roni hot on my heels. I reached and retched into the bowl with a fraction of a second to spare. At that precise moment, the countdown for the start of the show began. I knew I was the second guest on and set about cleaning myself up. I was well-practised in the art of vomiting without ruining my make-up, but wanted to get rid of the sour taste in my mouth. Roni fussed around getting me a glass of water, took me back into the green room and sat me down. I could tell from her forced expression – concern mixed with fear but over-laden with her usual steely determination – that she had finally realized that she had no choice but to tell me what was going on.

Less than ten minutes later I was sitting on a lavender blue L-shaped sofa between Gerry and Lil. 'So, Danny,' Gerry's voice was as smooth as his tanned complexion, 'we hear that you only had an hour's notice before being thrown in at the deep end last night to host "A Game of Two Halves".'

'And we also hear that you were *brilliant*!' Lil gushed unashamedly as she waved a tiny hand adorned with talon-like nails rather too near my face for my liking. Her small firm breasts and their pert nipples were alarmingly visible through a white silk blouse. Was this part of the openness that passed for sincerity in the world of television? 'You must have been *so* nervous.'

'But you behaved like a true professional,' Gerry simpered in a barely-disguised intimation that I was an amateur muscling in on his world. I felt Stella stirring, knowing that she wouldn't be able to ignore this type of goading, but used the whole force of my

Danny Devereux persona to control her. 'And we hear that you were an *enormous* hit with the ordinary viewers.'

'But what makes it all so much more special,' Lil lowered her voice as she grabbed my wrist in both her slender hands, moving as close to me as she could without her nipples touching me, 'is that we now hear that you went through *hell* to get here.'

'The traffic really wasn't that bad, Lil,' I grinned, pleased to have got a word in edgeways at last. Lil was, momentarily, lost for words.

In the green room just minutes earlier, Roni had admitted to the fabricated story Rex had leaked to the press that morning. I had, apparently, had a drug and drink dependency in the past from which Roni had saved me by paving the way for me to pour all my energy into the chirpy on-screen personality now evident to all. 'You'll appeal to your audience as a flawed, vulnerable, yet reformed character.' Roni had spouted Rex's PR spiel almost as fluently as he did. 'Think of the hope you'll give to all those in the same position whose lives have lost all meaning.' She chose not to notice me shaking my head in disbelief. I was far from convinced that I was saviour material but, as usual, hadn't been consulted. 'Now go on that sofa and show us what you're capable of!' She kissed me, but her lips felt cold against my cheek.

'Now put the jokes aside for a moment, Danny,' Lil's grip on my wrist tightened, 'and give yourself a bit of credit for your bravery and fortitude in turning your life around.'

'And proving that there's always hope,' Gerry grasped my other hand and I was surprised to find that his palm felt cool and clammy despite his glowing tan, 'no matter far down Skid Row you find yourself.'

Casting my mind back to these times causes me to hark back even further to the time in my childhood when I found religion – and the realization that an audience can be easily led to believe something if it genuinely wants to believe it. To say 'found' religion implies that I didn't know it was there, which I of course did. What I didn't know, until I started accompanying Sarah and her family to Our Lady of the Archangels, was that it was so *fascinating*. It's difficult to remember precisely what I thought the first time I attended Mass. It's like looking at an old black and white photograph of yourself and trying to recall your exact state of mind at the time. More than likely, you can't. And if you think you can, you're deluding yourself and therefore can't.

I do know that the orderliness impressed me. The way Sarah and her mother and father all knew to do a sort of half curtsey as they crossed the aisle (Sarah having helpfully explained in a rather loud whisper that the red candle beside the elaborate cupboard meant that Jesus was inside and demanded that we all perform this deferential bob) intrigued rather than intimidated me.

The priest's arrival also leaps to the fore when I tickle at the files of my memories. More specifically, it's what he was wearing that is imprinted firmly in my mind. Before he had made his shuffling entrance on what I was later to learn I wasn't to refer to as a stage, I had been taking in the unrestrained gaudiness of my surroundings.

Around the walls of the church hung unashamedly gilded paintings of Christ carrying his cross in various stages of pain and degradation. Hideous open wounds on his knees and back, apparently resulting from a sound flogging, and drops of blood oozing from lacerations around his head caused by the crown of thorns, were offset by the most elaborate and theatrical gold frames I had ever seen. They were, I later learned, Very Late Victorian Gothic, paid for, along with the rest of the church, by a local textile manufacturer intent on assuring his place in heaven (clearly either ignorant of or oblivious to the bible story I'd heard about camels and the eye of a needle). But that was later. Heaven and its feasibility and accessibility hadn't interrupted at this point. I moved on to looking at the altar, which was truly a glory for me to behold.

At home, my mother had embraced Seventies functionality as if by choice, even though it was by necessity because of her being wheelchair bound and needing to utilize all the domestic help they had in the art of making her immobility seem inconsequential rather than in cleaning unnecessary household adornments.

This church was the complete antithesis of our house and the altar – its crowning glory – was the most flamboyant thing I'd ever seen. It was carved from pink marble, edged in black marble, inset with what looked like solid gold and silver icons and backed by sumptuous curtains in red and gold brocade hanging from heavy brass rails.

Against this background, the priest arrived. Or rather, his vestments arrived. I noticed the priest inside them later. The heavy bright green and gold article of clothing could best be described as a rather unwieldy pinafore dress with various gold braided sashes and wonderfully elaborate shoulder pieces draped and tied around it. I was still marvelling at the amount of work in the fabric, when I noticed the priest's little head sticking out of the top. He looked like a surprised tortoise waking from hibernation to find his shell had been decorated like a carnival float. Quite innocently, I thought to myself that the only thing missing was his make-up. How could he go to all the trouble of getting dressed up and not finish the job off properly?

Later, I was very glad that I hadn't followed my instinct to whisper my thoughts to Sarah. Father Edmunds, with whom I was later to become very well acquainted, led the way swiftly and largely unintelligibly through the Mass. Sarah helpfully guided me with quietly spoken directions and explanations.

I didn't for one moment doubt the sincerity of Father Edmunds. I didn't doubt it because I had never for one moment supposed it was, or needed to be, there.

Before my next television appearance, I had managed to read up on my supposed dependencies and fit the symptoms and consequences into the illusory past that had been created for my invented character. Offers came in thick and fast enough for me to be unable to deny the fact that Roni and Rex had between them come up with a winning formula.

'What does it matter if it's not true, darling?' Three days had passed since the story had hit the media and I could see that Roni was bursting to tell me something. 'You've just been offered the rest of the run of "A Game of Two Halves"!'

My family, on hearing that I had become an altar boy under Father Edmunds' tutelage, somehow jumped to the collective conclusion – possibly aided and abetted by the discovery by one of my sisters of a small statue of the Virgin Mary in my bedroom – that I had set my sights on becoming a priest. When I think about what she was probably searching for, surely an effigy of a saint wasn't so bad?

'What a waste!' my mother was heard to wail. While I had no inclination towards or intention of being ordained, I resented the assumption that it would be a waste if I did. I was tempted to criticize the circular motion of their equine antics, but decided against it.

I was an altar boy for more than three years. Sarah was beside herself with jealousy, convinced that I must have categorically reserved my place in heaven while hers was still very much in the balance. Her parents were delighted, unashamedly claiming all the credit for my 'conversion'. Evidently they too were now closer to heaven as a result.

I think the only one who really knew why I did it was Father Edmunds. Without feeling threatened by my complete lack of faith – probably because his own had dissipated years earlier – he let me know that, more than appreciating my assistance, he had come to rely on it. I was always slightly ahead of him, always on the ball. I saw it as my role to make his, the leading one, easier. A slight squeeze from his shaking hand as we waited in the sacristy before Mass was enough to make me feel my presence was worthwhile. Every time I followed him through the heavy brocade curtains, I felt confident that I was instilling him with confidence. Everything had order and everything was in its place.

There was a live recording of 'A Game of Two Halves' in each of the five weeks that followed – weeks during which my previously-booked gigs became packed and any available nights were filled with new bookings. Needless to say, my price (or 'our' price) was inflated beyond my wildest dreams, but apparently not Roni's as she seemed to take it all in her stride, treating it as if it was inevitable and deserved.

Every night when we got home to that little flat in Battersea, we had a sort of ritual in which Roni made sure I went straight to bed while she made me a cup of herbal tea – or sometimes a mixture of Green and Earl Grey with lemon – which she would bring to me, then sit beside the bed and look at me as I drank it. Before long – after a prolonged bathroom ritual – she would join me in bed and we would drift off to sleep together. Or at least the idea was that we would drift off to sleep together. My mind used to be racing around with the happenings of the day and – more disturbingly – the potential happenings and disasters of the next; I couldn't help worrying about the possible reactions from audiences, the possibility of the magic running out.

Then in the sleepless early hours I would find myself snuggling closer to her sleeping form, listening to her breathing and wondering at the overwhelming waves of love I felt for her. She was my rock, my guide and my wife.

No matter how much she had cajoled, pushed and coerced me during the previous day, I felt any irritation and animosity towards her ebbing away in those dark hours, wondering how I had ever managed on my own.

It was much, much later that I discovered the true source of that feeling, that love I felt. By then I was too heavily embroiled, too involved, not to mention too married to do much about it. I still sometimes find myself regretting The Discovery.

My love for her – which I truly believed was mutual – made our daily chaotic schedules bearable and allowed me to build up my strength to put all the energy I had at my disposal into each 'Game' show. It seemed bizarre to me that a show formerly hosted by a macho ex-footballer who interviewed sports personalities on an equal footing was the vehicle for my television debut. Since I hadn't heard of most of them before reading the programme notes, I had unwittingly made the show my own by treating them as ordinary mortals, appealing to their human natures rather than their celebrity sporting ones and, in the process, acquired for the show a cult following for its comedy value.

An on-screen incident that stood out from others involved a large black footballer and a small Irish boxer who were guests on the same show. I made a genuine mistake and mixed up their professions.

'You really sail close to the wind,' the director said as the credits rolled, 'but you've got them eating out of the palm of your hand!'

'Of course he has!' Roni winked at me as she guided him away, knowing that I needed to be on my own. 'Now who've you got lined up for next week?'

I took a series of deep breaths, hoping that Roni would hurry up so that we could go home. There were too many people in the studio. Too many eyes. Too many mouths.

'God, you make me laugh.' One of the floor managers, whose name I couldn't remember, grinned as he rushed past. 'I was close to wetting myself!'

I was hilarious to watch.

But I was crying inside.

I didn't see it as a complicated process. It may have been terrifying, but it wasn't complicated. The basis of my interview technique was to ask wickedly personal questions I thought Iris would have asked with a deadpan look of enquiry on my face. Perhaps it would have been more complicated if I'd had to devise what I was going to do, how I was going to behave, but I hadn't had the luxury of time that first night. If I had, who knows what may or may not have happened?

Seeing each interview through to the end was far from easy, though, and there were times when I feared the audience wasn't with me. Without the audience on my side, the magic suddenly stopped working until I managed to grasp their attention back, elicit a laugh here, a snigger there, keep the delicate alchemy working.

'Ride from the seat of your pants, Daniel!' I still heard, from time to time, my mother's shouted words, which I can see now were intended to be encouraging. She may have lost her own mobility, but was determined to mobilize me in what she saw as the right direction. Was she successful?

'See how easily it's all falling into place!' Roni gleefully announced as the third 'Game' drew to a close. 'We're giving birth to a star.' I chose to keep my thoughts to myself – and struggled to quell a stirring Stella. There was nothing easy about what I was going through and whatever was in place was not there because it had fallen.

'What would she know about giving birth?' Stella's words remained internal thank God. 'Barren bitch!'

'Just be yourself.' Roni put her arm around me and I genuinely believed at that time that she was unaware of the extent of the agony she was putting me through. 'That's all you need to do, darling. Just be yourself.'

Sleep became more and more difficult to achieve as the days turned into weeks. Perversely, the resulting trance-like state in which I often found myself as I was propelled from comedy club to nightclub to television studio allowed the new 'me' to emerge and become a fully-fledged character in his own right. The stronger he became, the more he was able to keep Stella down in the depths from whence she came. I can't honestly say that I became confident, but I began to rely on this new persona to see me through. But see me through what? Did I honestly believe that, having launched her creation on the world, Roni would ever let me – or 'me' – rest? I must have believed it, in my astonishing naivety, or I wouldn't have been able to carry on.

Roni began to refer to 'The Tour' as if it was something we had discussed and formulated between us. She had booked thirty dates before I became aware that it was really going to go ahead. The biggest shock was that the first date was less than two weeks after the last 'Game' was aired.

'We have to strike while the iron's hot, darling,' she gushed. 'You *must* be able to see that.' Her face suddenly changed, her mouth turning down at the edges and a stricken look dulling the flashing sparkle in her eyes. 'Please don't tell me you don't want to do it. I don't think I could bear it.' I thought of the comfort of her sleeping form against mine and felt pangs of guilt at my ingratitude as she continued. 'I'm doing this for us, you know! Can't you see how many favours I've called in? I've practically had to *beg* to get some of these venues at such short notice. I agreed to be your manager and that's what I'm doing to the best of my ability!'

'I know you are!' I felt tears pricking behind my eyes as I realized I'd offended her. There was no denying the fact that I didn't want to be alone again. She didn't need to remind me that together we made a formidable team. 'It's just that I'm really tired and you keep taking me by surprise with your plans.'

'*Our* plans, darling.' She admonished me with a wagging index finger and a giggle. '*Our* plans.' I breathed a sigh of relief as I saw the smile return to her face. And I wasn't exaggerating about the tiredness. Sleep had become progressively harder to succumb to and I was operating in a lucid daze, often expecting to wake up any moment and find I was emptying paraffin from a dove pan into a back stage lavatory. 'Well, let's try and make sure you get a good night's sleep tonight, because we've got a meeting with the lawyers all day tomorrow to formulate the best structure for the production company.'

It was the first I'd heard about a production company and my heart sank at the thought of having to spend all day talking about it. As far as I was concerned, every waking hour needed to be spent formulating my act for The Tour which was looming closer like a ticking time bomb. Admittedly, since I was lucky if I slept for more than three hours a night, there were a lot of hours in which to do it, but I had to come up with a two hour one-man show which would appeal to audiences in locations as diverse and different as Norwich, Glasgow, St Albans and Cardiff. Roni, to her credit, had absolute faith in my ability to pull it off. But that wasn't enough in itself. I had to build up my fear, control it, learn to live with it and develop it into the sprightly on-stage patter that had to appear to come naturally.

'Did you hear me?' Roni caressed my upper arm gently. 'We've only got one day to sort out the structure for Danron Productions.'

'Yes.' I spoke quietly, not knowing what she expected me to say, not daring to tell her it was the first I'd heard of it. 'Forgive me if I'm being stupid, but why do we need one?'

'Need what?'

'A production company.'

'Darling, we've been through this so many times!' I knew that we hadn't. And she knew that I knew. The shape of her smile didn't waver, however, although its nature changed from benevolent to condescending in a split second as if her face had suddenly been cast into shadow. 'Do you truly trust me to manage your career in the way I best see fit?' Her top lip lifted slightly and the smile threatened to begin its transformation into a snarl. 'If you want me to back off and slow down, you only have to say.'

What could I say?

'Get back on that pony now!' I used to look up from the muddy ground in fear (of the hooves narrowly missing my face) and sadness (at the wheelchair bound control freak my mother had become). 'And don't you dare let me see you cry!'

'Oh my God! It's going to be so perfect!' Roni's face was alight as she came into the bedroom late one night a little over a week later with my tea in her hand and the cordless telephone clamped under her chin. I knew without asking that it was Rex on the other end. We had just arrived back from an exhausting gig in Brighton and I was really hoping that – for the first time in weeks – I would be able to get more than a few hours' sleep. Roni put the cup of tea on the bedside table and signalled for me to drink it, running a hand affectionately through my hair. 'We're happy to leave it in your hands Rex. And thanks for getting back to me so late at night.' She winked at me, hinting that she was about to share some good news. 'Ciao darling.' She ended the call, tossed the phone onto the bed, took both my hands in hers and looked for all the world like an excited child on Christmas Eve. 'We're going to have a spring wedding next year at Longdale Hall and,' she clapped her hands together and her eyes sparkled, 'it's going to be featured in OK magazine!'

'But Roni.' Not for the first time, it seemed that reality was slipping from my grasp. As at the lengthy discussions preceding the formation of Danron

Productions Limited the week before, I had a fleeting feeling that I was trespassing on someone else's life and was about to be revealed as an impostor. 'But Roni, we're already married.'

'I know darling, but this time it's going to be a *proper* wedding!' She put a hand gently to my face. 'Now drink your tea and try to get some sleep.'

The next day at the lawyer's office I signed the contract for The Tour, which in effect made me – or at least my performances – the property of the production company. 'It's just a formality darling.' Roni's apparent nonchalance before the event contrasted dramatically with her undisguised relief once the document was signed. 'It's nothing to worry about,' she said. I wasn't so sure. 'After all, *we* are Danron Productions aren't we? You might have signed your life away, but you've signed it away to yourself!' She laughed gaily and whisked it away before I could change my mind and grab it back from her.

'Just be yourself,' Roni said.

Two weeks later we moved out of the Battersea flat and put nearly all of our possessions in storage, the result of a battle I lost along with much of the precious little sleep I was getting anyway. 'It's illogical to spend money on accommodation we're not going to be living in.' Roni had broken the news gently while rubbing my shoulders in a musty dressing room at the Mean Fiddler. The audience that night had been particularly hard to win over, probably because their expectations had been raised by my television appearances. I felt completely exhausted and close to tears. The seven months of bookings around the country playing to audiences that promised to be hard to please loomed ahead of me. On top of that, I was now being faced with homelessness.

'But,' I leaned forward to sip my tea, 'I need to feel that I live somewhere. I need space in which to be myself. Even if I'm not there, I need to know where it is.'

'We simply can't afford it, darling.' She looked at me in the mirror, her reflection showing inverted sympathy. At least a part of every single day of the four years since she had become my manager had been spent planning The Tour and she wasn't going to let anything jeopardize it, least of all my quirky desire to have a home.

It's painful to remember my feelings the day we handed over the keys on a cold morning in February to a suited letting agent who had just finished an extremely impassive tour of the flat to check the state in which we were leaving it. Memories of the care and determination I had put into the personalization of each room threatened to erode the brave front I was determined to uphold.

'Come on, Danny!' Roni was standing behind the recently purchased car that was to be our means of transport for the months ahead. She was rearranging the last of our bags and suitcases in the open boot. 'What are you doing? We need to get going.'

'Just a minute,' I said quietly. 'I just need a minute.'

'What the bloody hell for?' She made no attempt to hide her annoyance, clearly unaware of the difficulty I was having saying goodbye to my sanctuary, the birth place of so much of my material, the safe haven to which I had retreated to shelter from the echoes of hostile audiences, the deeply personal and private space in which I had dissected recently-performed routines in order to decide what had worked and what most definitely hadn't. The most heart-rending aspect to the departure was, however, the fact that I felt – no, that I was terrified – that I would no longer feel close to the memory of my dear friend Iris. Without her remembered presence, how on earth would I manage to continue? 'For God's sake get a move on. We need to be in Northampton by lunch time for the technical rehearsal.' She slammed the boot shut noisily.

I looked up at the front of the building one last time, glanced sideways to the house where Iris had lived, then climbed solemnly into the passenger seat, feeling completely lost and out of control. Nothing would ever be the same again.

The Tour took us the length and breadth of the British Isles and involved me playing to audiences of all sizes and social backgrounds. On average, I did seven shows a week. Larger towns warranted a two-day stay, smaller ones just one night. Saturdays almost always involved two shows. On arrival in each town, sometimes even before we had found the hotel and unloaded our luggage, we went to the venue and did a technical rehearsal, which in itself was often enough to destabilize my already fragile endurance. As if the knowledge that I was soon to be in front of hundreds of people – many of whom were expecting me to do sports-based comedy because of my stint on 'A Game of Two Halves' and weren't reticent in showing their disappointment when I didn't – wasn't enough to contend with, I was also invariably faced with the harsh reality of unreliable sound systems, outdated lighting, incompetent staff and deplorable facilities. In one venue in the West Midlands, all backstage lavatory facilities were out of order, making it necessary for me to walk through the auditorium to use the front of house toilets.

It might sound as if I was becoming too hard to please, especially considering the venues I used to work in back in the Early Days, but the difference was that the expectations of my performance were so much higher now. The audiences were expecting – demanding even – to be entertained. If I was worrying about having to allow ten minutes for a lavatory visit just before the curtain went up, I wasn't concentrating on how to gauge the audience and deliver what they wanted.

Every audience was individual. To this day, I haven't properly defined the difference between London audiences and their provincial counterparts, but I'm sure it must have something to do with familiarity with live performance. The more accustomed they are to being entertained by the television, the more they are unwilling to react openly to what they see and hear. Working out what was going to entice them to give me enough reaction in order for me to give them more back in return was something that took all my energy in the first few minutes on stage. If I wasn't successful, the act was doomed to failure, like a car trying to run on an empty tank. Once I had worked out what they wanted and made them react, I could feed on their reaction and quench their thirst for more.

I have to admit that I wouldn't have been able to do it without Roni. But without her I wouldn't have been doing it in the first place. Everything we had, and a lot more we had borrowed thanks to Roni's unrelenting pushiness and drive, was resting on The Tour being a success. In retrospect, the extent to which she was gambling on my abilities would have made the task even more daunting if I had known about it. As it was, I let each day follow the one before, bounding through each set of curtains without a hint of the gut-wrenching fear of moments earlier permeating my performance. I had my battles to fight, Roni had hers. In some ways I suppose we were united in our quest, but I honestly don't think our aims ever coincided.

I suppose I could speculate on what would have happened to us if success hadn't been part of the bigger picture. How long would she have persevered with me? As I was to discover later, I wasn't her first protégé, but I must have been the first over which she had virtually total control. I know it constantly occurred to me on that gruelling tour that I would rather be somewhere else, but I had got to the point where I didn't know where that was.

After all, I had nowhere to call home any more. In addition, if I had ever known who I was and what I needed in order to exist, I certainly didn't now. Roni had been the catalyst for the partial metamorphosis that had left me in this limbo-like state. She was the only constant in my daily existence. I had no fixed abode. I no longer had the daily appearance of my alter-egos. Almost every day I was faced with a different venue, which inevitably involved a different pair of curtains. Was it any wonder that I became her acquiescent acolyte?

Now I've had time to think about it, I honestly believe that Roni couldn't see anything wrong in what she was doing. For her, things were far more straightforward. Her faith that her efforts would reap rewards was admirably unswerving. And of course they eventually did in the form of the Big Break.

Tonight's outfit is the Vivienne Westwood creation Roni wore for our second wedding. I've got the clippings from OK magazine to make sure I get the make up right. In fact, I've taken a bit longer than usual laying out the required items. I don't want to get complacent just because the plan – my plan – has so far gone perfectly to schedule.

Another body – this one reported to have been in the river for four days – was retrieved this morning. I still find it impressive that a pathologist can work out details like that. But then a pathologist would no doubt find it impressive that I can become someone else in the blinking of an eye (or so it appears). 'The body is of a young male in his twenties bearing a newly tattooed letter E on his chest' according to the BBC news. The tattoo on the body will not have begun to heal, unlike the corresponding letter on my forearm, which has formed another inky scab. I gently rub Vaseline on them every night and force myself to resist the temptation to scratch.

Tonight's Night Visitor will be labelled with an 'I' – carefully chosen so as not to be confused with an 'L' – provided he doesn't change his mind and not turn up. That of course has been the potential flaw in my plan all along. The positive effect of the worry that this causes is that it, albeit momentarily, brings some relief from the practically endless question of the divide between murder and suicide.

Is it truly a crime to succumb to being anything other than yourself – or is it only a crime if you lose yourself as a result?

The Big Break

C

The day of the Big Break began as did many others while we were on the road. I woke up exactly five minutes before the alarm went off, climbed quietly out of our shared bed being careful not to wake Roni and walked to the window to draw back the curtains, which were of a garish geometrical design in shades of green and yellow, giving you an idea of the type of hotel to which our means stretched at the time. The town I saw below looked much the same as many others and, as happened quite often, I couldn't immediately put a name to the place.

A shopping street stretching out below the hotel was alarmingly indistinguishable from similar streets in many other towns due to the foothold grasped by branches of huge national chains. From that window I could see, amongst others, a Tesco, a Boots, a WHSmith, a Dixons and a McDonalds, looking with their immediately recognizable shop fronts like predators grown fat from the consumption of their numerous smaller predecessors. Grey and blue tiled roofs stretched for miles in each direction, punctuated by a church steeple here, an ugly tower block there and a factory with a smoking chimney in the far distance.

I recall – or think I recall – that on that morning I was feeling particularly ungrounded. The constant moving from town to town performing in unfamiliar venues had left me feeling that I lived nowhere, that I belonged nowhere, that I was struggling to swim in a foreign sea way out of my depth. I couldn't help myself from reminiscing about my days in the flat in Battersea. While I can't pretend that life there had been perfect, the sense of balance I had acquired while living in that tiny flat had now completely disappeared. What I definitely remember is that I couldn't see a way out of the predicament in which I had found myself.

I looked out of the window again at the collection of grey buildings below me. Still unable to put a name to the town and unaware of the significance the day ahead was going to assume, I went quietly into the bathroom.

As always, I softened my beard with hot water before moving on to clean my teeth, first with an inter-dental brush then an electric toothbrush, making sure I used a minimum of one hundred and eighty vertical strokes on each tooth, moving away from the gums. I then applied shaving gel and left it for one hundred and fifty seconds. This is still part of my daily routine – it enables a much closer shave and particularly helps with the tricky bristles that try to hide at the entrance to my nostrils. Even now, when I never go outside, I don't feel happy with allowing the day to begin until my face is smooth and clean.

As I came out of the bathroom, our breakfast arrived. Roni looked eagerly at the waiter bringing it in to see if he recognized me. It was possible, of course, because she was relentless in her drive to make me famous: the local press, television and radio stations quite often gave in to the bombardment to which she subjected them and interviewed me. It was from these that she used to glean the quotes she used on the posters, flyers and advertisements for The Tour (along with the now very well-used ones from 'A Game of Two Halves'). But he put the tray of coffee, cereal and toast down on the melamine bedside cabinet without a hint of recognition.

As I said, it started off as just an ordinary day on the road. Yet another ordinary day before I was a household name.

I never underestimated Roni's ability to make things happen. Mind you, neither did she, or they wouldn't have. Nevertheless, when the somewhat commonplace looking duo arrived at my dressing room with her just after the show that day, I didn't initially pay them any heed. Roni frequently introduced me to people with whom I had very little in common. I invariably managed to be civil on these occasions, but rarely found them enjoyable. 'Danny, I'd like you to meet Tim Paisley and Amanda Blyton.' I stood up and noticed that Tim bore a striking resemblance to Cliff Richard and Amanda had a cleverly-bleached but distinctly heavy moustache. I couldn't help getting the impression that Roni expected me to know who they were.

'How do you do?' I shook hands with both of them and wondered what they wanted. The gleam in Roni's eye should have told me something, but I was allowing myself not to pay too much attention. For half an hour or so after I came off stage, I needed to make the transition gently. Like waking from a deep sleep to complete consciousness, I couldn't negotiate it in a hurry. So is it any wonder that I was caught off guard when a day that had started as just an ordinary day on the road ended with me being offered a television series of my own?

'It'll be a co-production between SpotCheck TV – our company – and Danron Productions,' Amanda explained patiently. 'We've already pre-sold the idea for the series to the BBC. An option on a second series is part of the deal.'

I suppose I was meant to ask eager questions about the terms of this milestone, this goal towards which they clearly assumed I must have been pushing myself for my entire career up to this point. They were probably, I now realize, anticipating me to enquire about the financial rewards I was to reap. Instead, I remained silent. Looking back, I can only imagine what my facial expression betrayed as I struggled with the sense of impending doom that was steadily beginning to take hold.

'Danny?' Roni tried unsuccessfully to keep the annoyance out of her voice.

'Shall we leave you to discuss it with Roni?' Tim looked at me with a mixture of concern and amusement. My lack of reaction had obviously surprised him. He was, no doubt, having difficulty reconciling the exuberant life form he had just seen perform on stage (not, I was later to discover, for the first time as he, Amanda and various BBC executives had seen the whole show on no less than thirty occasions) and the subdued, bewildered, silent person here in the dressing room.

'Why don't we see you at our hotel at, say, ten in the morning?' Amanda said hurriedly and handed Roni a card.

'Fine!' Roni chirped gratefully. 'I'll come out with you. I need a word with the House Manager before we leave anyway.' She shot me a backward glance as she left. 'Back in five minutes, darling.'

I later found that detailed negotiations with SpotCheck – along with half a dozen other interested production companies – had been going on for months. But I didn't know that as she arrived back in the prescribed five minutes brandishing a bottle of Veuve Clicquot and a couple of glasses. 'We've done it!' She splashed champagne into the glasses, handed me one, clinked hers against it and then drank it down in one. 'We've bloody well done it!' She hurled herself at me with arms outstretched and hugged me tight, jumping up and down as she did. Was it pure joy she was feeling or triumph?

'But we've only got until ten in the morning to discuss it.' I wanted to feel as elated as she did, but had nagging doubts and fears. I had only survived the tour so far by the skin of my teeth. There was no way I was ready for television.

'What is there to discuss?' The line of Roni's jaw tightened as her suspicion was confirmed that my reaction was not altogether positive. I had thought (obviously wrongly) that I would be allowed to express an honest opinion as I wasn't in front of an audience. Her assumption that I would go along with her wishes yet again gave me the courage to speak out.

'For goodness' sake, Roni, we need to talk this through and think about what we're letting ourselves in for before we commit to—'

'You don't deserve a career!' Her glass smashed noisily on the floor. 'I can't believe you're even questioning this chance in a million.' She brought the back of her hand across her face to wipe away a tear. 'Above all, you don't deserve *me*!'

This seemed fairly plausible to me, but I didn't dare say so. Maybe, I realized suddenly, it was good old fashioned fear that had caused my reaction. Or maybe she would believe that it was. Either way, I *was* genuinely scared of the irrevocable situation into which I had got myself. 'Roni, I'm scared!' I raised my voice – except that it was actually 'my' voice – and matched her tears with my own.

'Darling!' She softened immediately and threw her arms around me again, grasping my shoulders gently and pushing me away from her so she could look (with concern) into my tear-stained face. 'I *know* you're scared. I am too.'

'I don't want to let you down,' I simpered, matching her tone perfectly. 'What if I mess it up? After all your hard work, I could lose our contract, our television show...' My voice trailed off and I allowed a few more tears to flow. I could see Roni's recognition of the fact that I had said 'your' followed by 'our' and I had used each term twice. It had worked a treat and she swallowed it hook, line and sinker.

But then I couldn't think of a way to get out of signing the television contract the next day.

By the night of the Big Break, I was just about getting used to 'being myself'. Creating that new and, by necessity, consistent persona had taken more work than all the other characters I used to work with put together. All I had to hide behind was the need to keep it consistent and stick to the tree I'd created. However far I meandered along one of its branches, whether an old one or one that had sprouted on the spur of the moment, I could dart back to the trunk and be safe, as long as I'd constructed the tree to be strong, supportive and – above all – naturally invisible. What I couldn't do was suddenly become another character, another voice, another person. I had to be 'me': the new persona I had been forced to create.

It helped that the character had been built on the premise that all I had to do was think about what Iris would do or say in a given situation, then adapt it to come out as if I had said it naturally. But sometimes I just couldn't connect with her and I used to feel a blind panic rising in my chest, followed by a shortness of breath, then a hot flush and a cold sweat – usually just before I went on and was staring at the back of a set of curtains.

This was always the worst time. I could visualize the audience on the other side, waiting to devour me, but hopefully destined to throw back enough entrails with which I could put enough of myself back together to devour *them*. But they didn't know the process involved; they had, after all, just come to watch a show. And they didn't know how I was feeling as I waited on the other side. And Roni didn't know the hell I went through as I looked at the back of those curtains.

In civic centres, they were usually constructed of strange man-made fibre in various shades of beige. It was encouraging to occasionally encounter genuine velvet. In a small Victorian theatre that had just been refurbished – and was very nearly a delight to work in – they were brand new and fashioned from burgundy velvet with heavy gold tasselled trimmings. More often, though, the curtains were old and moth eaten, their linings full of holes. From the audience's point of view they would look fine, but I could see that they were about to fall apart.

The Tour continued after the day of the Big Break for just over three months, during which time Roni changed almost beyond recognition. She seemed to become something, or someone, she had been waiting to be all along. Everything had to now revolve around the impending television show. Why on earth, I asked myself, did there need to be so many meetings? Being on tour gave me enough to worry about on a daily basis without Roni and her new television cronies banging on and on about material and content and censorship.

'He can't follow a rigid script,' she insisted at one meeting. She was wearing a version of what had become her new uniform: sharply-cut trouser suits worn with exquisite designer high heels and – always – perfectly manicured nails painted to match the colour of the shoes. She was surely and steadily building up a collection of large sunglasses which, I have to admit, suited her. She had been my manager for a long time. Now she truly looked the part – the cold, hard, calculating tigress who would kill to protect her client. 'It'll kill the uniqueness of his—'

'But no-one works without a script,' Amanda Blyton interjected.

'I know that!' Roni snapped.

'What we need to ensure,' Tim Paisley, ever the peace-keeper, waved his hand gently between them, 'is the consistency of Danny's essential essence.'

They discussed me as if I were a tangible and measurable commodity, something that could be marketed in the same way as deodorant or after-shave. Then I realized that I was fast becoming just such an entity. They took me apart, swapped my innards around and stitched me back up again (speaking metaphorically of course, or is it allegorically?) They had bought me being myself – or so they thought – so why were they already trying to change me before the series had even begun? Thank God they didn't know what a construct this 'me' was or they might have had to have more meetings about the fundamental nature of the product in which they were investing.

The one advantage of all this was that it kept Roni busy. And when she was busy, she was off my back. And when she was off my back, it made it easier to ensure that she never saw me vomit with fear as I waited behind the curtains for a show to begin.

When The Tour finally came to an end, Roni rented us a flat in Soho, which she later maintained was completely my idea. The flat itself was pleasing enough, if a little noisy, and proved to be a good place for me to work on the essential new material for the television show. The front window, with its slightly incongruous Liberty print festooned blinds, overlooked a street with a mixture of gay bars, restaurants, sex shops and a theatre. The little roof terrace at the back, accessed through French windows framed with swags-and-tails curtains in the same Liberty design, was almost entirely surrounded by chimneys and air-conditioning units. The only possible breach of our privacy was from a small window a floor higher, but I never saw its off-white net curtains move.

The pleasure of once again having somewhere to call home went some of the way towards allaying my fears of the television show as it loomed closer. There was a tangible feeling of anticipation in that little flat with its reproduction furniture at which we could smile condescendingly because we hadn't chosen it. There was a highly polished reproduction Regency sleigh bed (complete with artificial wood worm holes). We used to jump up and down on it and pretend we were newlyweds trying it out in a bed showroom, working out how long it would take us to save up for it.

When I remember little episodes like that I feel sad. The reason for my sadness is not that we were happy and lost that happiness. I have realized that my sadness is rooted in the fact that – before The Discovery – I genuinely believed that I was in love with Roni.

To say I was happy during the days in the Soho flat would probably be exaggerating, since I can't remember ever being simply happy, but I do remember an all-pervading sense of wellbeing. Roni was out at meetings a lot, leaving me to do my revision and work on new material, which she would then fight to have included in one of the shows. Every so often, I went to a meeting with her, but on the whole I was left to my own devices. I would look forward to her coming home, quite often telling myself when she was later than expected that, if I filled the kettle as full as I could then switched it on and off and on again, I would hear her key in the door by the time it had boiled.

When she eventually did come home – never, I hasten to admit, coinciding with the kettle boiling – we would drink our tea and, more often than not, end the evening dragging each other to that fake-worm-holed bed.

Despite much retrospective analysis, there is no doubt in my mind about my love-stricken state at that time. She allowed me to believe that she was entirely responsible for the feeling of contentment that resulted. She hinted that without her I was worth nothing. With her, she told me repeatedly whether wordlessly or not, I could develop the saleable commodity that would otherwise have remained hidden deep within.

During that planning time, that hiatus between The Tour and The Television Show, I made my intentions perfectly clear to Roni. For obvious reasons, I need to be absolutely sure that I was never guilty of misleading her. I can honestly say, albeit it to myself, that I wasn't. On more occasions than I can possibly count, I clearly expressed the fact that I had severe doubts about a television career and didn't want her to build up any false hopes. The conversation I remember most vividly took place very early one morning after I had spent a sleepless night literally paralyzed with fear at the prospect of the task ahead. She had come home the night before full of excitement because of a meeting she had just attended about drawing up an option for a second series.

'Roni,' I said quietly when I felt her stir and saw her open one eye, 'I really don't want to let you down, but I don't feel confident that I can deliver the goods you're promising. More than that, I don't feel safe. I'm worried that I'll completely lose—'

'You're just nervous because you're moving out of your comfort zone,' she interrupted sternly, sitting up in bed so that she could look down on me. Her voice softened to a gentle purr as she continued. 'Darling, it's essential that you push your boundaries. I'm here to look after you, to allow you to take one step at a time. Let's get the first series under our belts before you make decisions about the second.'

'I can't imagine there being a second series,' I said honestly. 'I'm not exaggerating when I say that I don't think—'

'Nerves!' She laughed. 'Just nerves! You'll be fine!'

My sentiments were clearly not to her liking so, in her usual fashion, she modified them in her own mind. Perhaps I should have tried harder to tell her what I was truly feeling. If that's the case, then I have to hold myself at least partly responsible. It's clear now that, once the series was underway and successful, she chose to completely forget my misgivings and assume they had disappeared. My diligent drive to get through the series without losing my mind was obviously seen as an admission of my unconditional acquiescence with her demands. She had secured the contract. My part of the bargain was to come up with the goods, do the shows and insinuate myself into the hearts and minds of the public. I was 'our' commodity. I was the property of Danron Productions.

Tonight's outfit is a white linen Chanel suit, which I will wear with bright pink patent leather Manolo Blahniks. I worked on the gel nails all afternoon – which are in the same candy tones as the shoes – not wanting to rush them and make the overall effect anything less than perfect. It sounds like a frivolous outfit, but I can assure you that frivolity is far from the emotion it inspires in me.

I can remember her wearing this outfit on the day I made The Discovery.

Part of me wouldn't mind not having known that my love was chemically induced – the same part of me that thinks that feelings matter more than their source. After all, I've made my living from appearing to be other people. What is honest about that? So why does honesty matter so much to me?

A pair of Versace sunglasses, their white frames studded at the sides with pink stones, will be worn beneath the severely bobbed coiffure to complete the look. Tonight's Night Delivery won't be able to see 'her' eyes. The ink, the needle and the letter 'C' – which I took from the book of Exodus in an American Family Bible dated 1859 – are lined up ready for their part in the charade.

While I personally still have a problem coming to terms with the fact that this is yet another human being who has decided that life is not worth living, Veronica Bedford will be cold, hard and calculating as she executes the task.

The TV Show & The Discovery

A

That Roni had planned our Spring wedding – complete with OK magazine coverage – well before The Big Break seemed to serve as proof, at least to her, that we were following our true destiny. The jagged pieces of the jigsaw, which she and she alone had always known were part of a coherent plan, were finally fitting together. To the impartial observer, it may have appeared that we were a couple destined for and deserving of great things. I knew it was a result of her determination and sheer ruthlessness. But why do I of all people need to draw attention to the fact that appearances can and frequently do deceive?

The venue for the celebration was Longdale Hall, a beautiful mansion of Jacobean origins owned by one of Roni's acquaintances. He was one of only three people she referred to as such, none of whom I had met before this second wedding. When their significance became apparent, I came to think of them as The Acquaintances. What it took me a little longer to grasp was that they were all men whom Roni had dated and subsequently tried to manage before she finally found me. When this fact became startlingly apparent to me, the realization brought with it, along with the knowledge that I had been led along like a blinkered donkey, a clammy nauseous sensation not dissimilar to seasickness. It rocked the foundations of my already unstable world and marked the beginning of the end of my love affair with my wife.

The first of The Acquaintances was – and still is – a composer with whom many of you will be familiar. He struggled in the commercial arena before meeting, falling in love with and marrying Rowena Fullmore, the daughter of a Midlands property magnate whose inherited wealth enabled her to pander to her husband's creative whims. An expert gardener, she planted the grounds of their house in Norfolk with the particular aim of inspiring his classical works. They apparently still hold regular recitals and concerts in this showpiece arena garden, alongside an annual festival to showcase the works of new composers.

'She looks like a fucking horse,' Roni whispered, jerking her head in Rowena's direction as we walked into the tiny chapel to re-affirm our vows. 'Never mind the bloody Arts Council funding they get for their festival, she ought to be sponsored by the Jockey Club.'

It was Rowena herself who told me a little later that Roni, during their courtship, had tried to persuade Jonathan – the composer – to write stage musicals. Her lip curled back in amusement from her substantial front teeth as she told me. 'I mean, what was she thinking?' Her question was accompanied by a barely-perceptible snort. 'She must have been able to see that Jonathan was born to write classical symphonies not that commercial audience fodder.' She threw back her head to laugh, blissfully unaware of the off-putting nature of her cavernous mouth. 'No doubt she was picturing herself as that Brightman creature next to him as Lloyd-Webber.' This time the snort was unmistakable. I smiled politely as she put her hand on my arm. 'She's got her hands full managing *you* now though, I should imagine!' With that, she trotted off towards a waiter bearing a tray of full champagne glasses.

You may well wonder why this was the first time I had met any of The Acquaintances, but there's not really any mystery involved. It was entirely due to the fact that Roni wanted to show off to them, now that she felt she had finally made it and was worthy of their company. I imagine they were all a bit bemused – or perhaps even afraid – when she got in touch to invite them, but curiosity had obviously won through and even led to one of them being coerced into lending us his house and garden for the ceremony and reception, although it transpired that adultery and OK magazine had also played a large part in this.

The second Acquaintance is a novelist now reaping the rewards of his fifth bestseller and currently working on the screenplay of the second of his novels to be turned into a motion picture. At the time of the second wedding, he was just emerging as an eminent literary voice following the recent publication of his first novel, which had apparently taken seven years to write.

'I bet he's not going to admit that the inspiration for that book came from me,' Roni hissed as she watched the photographer from OK snapping away around him. 'Without me he'd still be doing restaurant reviews in the Sunday supplements.' She nibbled her lip and I wondered why she had invited a guest who clearly made her so angry. 'And you can be sure there won't be another novel to follow that one!' This wedding day, which was meant to be about affirming our love for each other in public, was fast becoming a series of revelations about Roni's past. The more I discovered, the more nervous I became.

And that brings me to the third Acquaintance, of whose hospitality we were availing ourselves that day. He was – or at least had been at the time they agreed to cover the wedding – the main attraction and bait used to reel in OK magazine. Having several times been voted by the readers of popular magazines as one of the top five actors with whom your average woman in the street would like to have a sexual encounter (whether the questions were worded that way or not), he was married to an equally popular soap actress. Together, they had been awarded the accolade 'Most Envied Celebrity Couple' (or the couple with whom your average couple in the street would most like to put their swinging fantasies to the test).

Clever old Rex Avalon, ever with his ear to the ground and nose sniffing for scandal, had got hold of the rumour that the couple were going through a bad patch purported to be as a result of a slight indiscretion with a swarthy member of an Irish boy band. He approached OK magazine with the idea, then presented the thespian couple with an attractive proposal: they host a wedding for a friend at their gorgeous mansion and show the world (via the magazine) what a happy, well-rounded, devoted and generous couple they were, simultaneously stamping on any rumours of infidelity and discord. It's not rocket science; it's how Rex Avalon has been earning his living for years. More often than not, it works.

Following the deal being struck, I had then become something of a success myself, which made the magazine exposure (timed to coincide with the beginning of the television series) convenient, well-timed and – Roni wasn't averse to claiming – prophetic.

Looking over at our hosts who were hand in hand and glowing with celebrity coupledom (even though I subsequently found out that the boy band rumour was true and that it was him not her who was the participant in the imprudent dalliance), Roni's lip curled back in the beginnings of a snarl. 'Look at them playing Lord and Lady Bountiful!' I couldn't help feeling that she was being rather ungrateful, but I could sense that there was more to come. I could see a pattern forming. 'Without me, he'd never have got through the audition for the part that launched his television career.' The role to which she was referring was – I am no doubt you are already aware – that of a young maverick policeman whose unorthodox methods infuriated his superiors but never failed to solve the crime. The signature scar on his cheek, I was to discover quite a lot later, was an indelible reminder of a vicious fight – involving a whisky glass – with Roni the night before the audition. 'But don't worry darling, we're going to make it in our own right now and leave them all standing!'

The bigger picture was revealing itself to me. And I didn't like what I saw.

The actual ceremony was held in the chapel: a tiny, exquisite and eminently photogenic structure attached to the house by an ancient carved stone cloister that led onto a lush lawn. A fountain depicting three entwined nymphs shot a jet of water into the air. This was backed by a white garden, inspired apparently by Vita Sackville-West's legendary creation at Sissinghurst, fronted by a ha-ha allowing the lawn to meld seamlessly with rolling parkland dotted with magnificent mature oaks and cedars. The white drawing room – where the reception was to be held – opened directly onto the lawn, its white damask curtains flapping gently at the open French windows in the slight breeze.

The weather was as perfect as is possible on an early April day in Hampshire. Fears expressed by the stylists, photographers, caterers and – not least – our hosts proved to be ill-founded. My biggest worry was that I would be expected to socialize. That too proved to be somewhat ill-founded since the entire event was for the benefit (and not forgetting at the expense) of the magazine. It was really just an elaborate photo shoot populated with choice celebrities; Rex had brought a few of his clients and Ellie had collared two of her hottest properties. Throughout the whole day, however, I only really conversed with The Acquaintances.

The Novelist was first. He waited until Roni had flounced off in her Vivienne Westwood creation before he sidled up to me discreetly. He had one of those faces which – through its almost complete lack of expression – made you think there was a lot going on beneath the surface. It's what Iris said first attracted her to me. 'Congratulations,' he said quietly. I didn't know exactly at what his good wishes were aimed. It could have been the first wedding, the second wedding or the imminent television series.

'Thank you,' I said, shaking his proffered hand rather awkwardly, 'your book seems to be making quite an impression.' We were in the doorway leading from the drawing room out to the white garden. When the OK spread came out, one of the photos showed the two us framed by the white curtains caught mid billow in the slight breeze: the newly-acclaimed novelist beside the up-and-coming chat show host frozen in mid conversation for posterity.

'Don't forget,' he spoke slowly and deliberately, 'that your talent is yours.' He swallowed awkwardly and paused to add weight to his next utterance. 'Uniquely yours.'

Roni appeared beside us – too late for that particular photograph – and clapped her hands together delightedly.

'So good to see you boys getting on so well!' She put an arm around each of us and smiled encouragingly, apparently oblivious to the fact that her arrival had succeeded in ending our brief conversation.

A little while later, I was approached by The Composer and his wife. 'Congratulations.' She spoke first, having obviously decided that it wasn't enough to have already filled me in on the past her husband and my wife had in common, then descended on me with a toothy kiss to both cheeks. 'We'd both like to wish you all the best in your life together.'

'Yes,' he shook my hand firmly and, I thought, conveyed a mixture of sympathy and relief in the gesture. 'It's a tough business you're in. I hope you've got what it takes to survive it.'

'Of course he has,' Rowena gushed, 'with a partner in crime like Roni!' A little whinny came out as she laughed.

'Yes,' her husband said quietly with a barely perceptible shake of his head.

Finally, The Actor took his turn, cornering me by the fountain for a casually purposeful photo opportunity, consistently ensuring that his scarred cheek was towards the camera. He grasped my hand and clapped me on the shoulder, throwing in a trademark wink. 'You're a brave man,' he said with forced jocularity.

'She's not that frightening really!' It was my turn to force the humour. My weak laugh petered out. I cleared my throat. 'I really can't thank you enough for your hospitality.'

'You are more than welcome Danny.' His smile, clearly well-rehearsed, didn't reach his eyes. He opened his mouth as if to speak again, but must have thought better of it as his wife floated with an enviable nonchalance into the camera's range. 'Ah, here's Melanie.' Was it really possible that he thought I hadn't seen her?

'Congratulations Danny.' She kissed me dutifully on both cheeks as the photographer performed his task, then seemed to be wondering what to say next. If I could have read her mind, I would probably have seen that she was working out how much longer all these people had to be cluttering up their house and garden.

'Thank you.' My mind struggled to find something else to say. It failed. After a few moments spent in awkward silence, she suddenly raised her hand to wave at someone on the other side of the lawn, squeezed my hand and wandered off, leaving me with her husband, who cleared his throat purposefully.

'Beware of the tea.' He looked fearfully over his shoulder as he said it.

'What?'

'Roni's tea. Don't drink too much of it.' With that, he too seemed to see someone on the far side of the lawn urgently needing his company. 'I'll speak to you later, Danny.' Another trademark wink and he was gone.

He didn't speak to me later.

Looking back now, I think it was probably anxiety that the television series – this pinnacle of her achievement – wouldn't be the success that she so desperately needed that caused the change in Roni. It is also possible that she had been holding her real personality in check before and was now simply allowing herself to become the person she really was. The role of wife/manager seemed to have been made for her and she genuinely appeared to relish every moment. While I couldn't wait to get home to the little Soho flat so that I could be myself rather than 'myself', Roni was the same whether in public or private, whether it was day or night. I think she probably spent her sleeping hours dreaming about deals, contracts and the new heights she could aim for and reach.

It's a bizarre irony that after The Shooting several newspapers – one in particular – cast Roni as the wronged wife, sympathizing with her for having stood by me on my journey to success, sacrificing her own dreams in favour of being (I quote) 'the wind beneath my wings'. How appearances can deceive, often on purpose.

She still used to make me a cup of tea every night, but (unbeknown to her) I never drank one after the second wedding.

The format of the television show was quite straightforward. I had an hour during which to interview two guests and incorporate a bit of topical comment laced with witty, off-the-cuff comedy. I'm still not sure how confident Roni was that it would work. What I do know – without the slightest shadow of a doubt – is that it wouldn't have worked without the monumental effort on my part, which was a direct result of the paralyzing fear I felt at the thought of the task ahead of me. If it's true that the fear of success is greater than the fear of failure – and I am in no way refuting the theory – you could ask why I pushed so hard to make it such a triumph. I could, you might say, have made sure the show was a miserable disappointment and saved myself all the trouble that was ahead.

So I suppose I had better tell you why I didn't.

First of all, I wasn't capable of seeing into the future.

Secondly, I had been completely thrown off balance by the discovery of Roni's stash of class A drugs. The Discovery confirmed my suspicions and put paid to any hope that my love for her – and the stabilizing effect that it supplied – could ever return.

Thirdly, the set for the television series didn't have curtains.

So the answer to the question is not complicated: I needed the challenge the television show provided to keep me from descending into the depths of despair.

When the credits rolled after the first show – the first of eighteen in the series – Roni threw her arms around me, hugged me tight and planted what would have seemed to an onlooker genuine kisses all over my quivering face. I had pushed myself harder than I would have thought possible. Gut-wrenching fear had enabled 'me' to overplay the nonchalant irreverence for which I was to become so famous, launching volleys with no guarantee that they would be returned. Needless to say, they were returned, leading to more being launched and returned in turn. The risk paid off and the audience lapped it up enthusiastically.

'I *knew* you could do it! It's unique!' Her praise seemed to belittle what I had done. Did she have any idea how I felt inside? 'We're going to have guests queuing up to come on the show now!' She squeezed my hand as she pulled me towards the sound of champagne corks popping. 'We've made it!' She said the words without turning to look at my face.

It was during one of my sleepless nights a few days before the first television show that I discovered the capsules. I had been looking for sleeping tablets – an abundance of which I knew she possessed and with which she had been dosing herself that same night. That she too had trouble sleeping perhaps contradicts the front she managed to keep up at all times: that of the cool, confident manager completely in control. I knew she had anxieties, deep-seated fears, perhaps even a sense of self-loathing that drove her on to high achievement. These qualities had contributed towards the love I had developed for her, but not as much as – it now transpired – these chemicals with which she had been lacing my nightly cup of tea.

Since the unsolicited advice of the thespian Acquaintance at our second wedding, I had found different ways of avoiding the evening brew and had noticed that I no longer felt the warmth, longing and unconditional nocturnal affection for my wife. Owing to the fact that I had very little time to think of anything other than the gruelling trauma ahead of me – and all the expectations it brought with it – I had tried to put the matter from my mind, almost convincing myself that I was paranoid and perhaps reacting to the stress of being a celebrity. I couldn't overlook, however, that our sex life had fizzled away to nothing and, more to the point, I couldn't deny that it was because I no longer found her attractive.

Hidden at the back of her make-up cabinet, the capsules were in a jam jar brazenly labelled 'MDMA' in red marker on the lid. The quest for sleeping tablets and the longed-for oblivion they would induce was pushed out of my mind by the return of my suspicions. I padded quietly to Roni's desk, switched on her computer and logged onto the internet.

Methylenedioxymethamphetamine, I learned, was first synthesised and patented by a drug company in Germany in 1914 and was designed as an appetite suppressant. Sixty years later it was given to psychotherapy patients because it helped them to open up and talk about their feelings. This custom stopped abruptly in 1986 when animal studies showed that it could cause brain damage.

The main ingredient of the rave drug known as 'Ecstasy', it apparently induces a wide range of feelings and emotions. There was no shortage of information on numerous internet sites. One sentence in particular leapt out at me from the screen. *'The most similar experience familiar to most people is being in love.'*

'But it worked didn't it?' Roni's shameless honesty and refusal to even attempt to deny her actions completely took the wind out of my sails. I wanted to tell her that I felt deceived, that she had used me, that my emotions weren't something that could be played with. 'So are you telling me,' she continued, 'that when you said you loved me you didn't mean it?'

Does a painting thought to be by an Old Master – as such holding great value – then subsequently discovered to be a clever fake still retain any residual value?

A photograph of Roni and me at our first wedding hangs above the desk in Roni's study. I can't help glancing up at it from time to time as I work on the letter for tonight's tattoos. I can't put my hand on my heart and say that I would rather not have ever been in love.

But it doesn't make what she did any less forgivable.

From having worked nearly every night of the week for years, I suddenly found I was in front of an audience – albeit a much larger one – only once a week. Far from feeling that this signalled that I had made it, I felt like a fish out of water. The first television series proved three things to me: that I *could* do live television, that I *hated* doing live television and that, without curtains to come through onto the set, I didn't know my arse from my elbow and was in danger of completely losing control.

I first realized the extent of my celebrity status – or 'our' celebrity status as Roni liked to refer to it – when we actually caught a reporter going through our rubbish. I don't know what he expected to find, but what he did find could only have reinforced our public image as a normal and happy celebrity couple. Depending on what could be classed as 'normal' and 'happy', nothing could have been further from the truth.

'What?' Roni's eyes almost popped out of their sockets. We had arrived at the television studio on South Bank as we always did just over three hours before the show – the sixth one of the series – went on air. The plain white clinical walls of the dressing room were closing in on me as they had on the five previous occasions. There was no hint of the performance that was to come, there was no distant hum of a hungry crowd, no smoky atmosphere out of which I would conjure my magic. 'Please tell me this is your idea of a sick joke.'

'I'm not joking, Roni. I simply can't do it. I can't go on.' I took a deep breath. ' They'll have to find a replacement.'

I have to admit that I hadn't concocted this confrontation on my own. Following my discovery of the level to which Roni had been controlling my emotions, I had been less inclined to suppress Stella's appearances. To be honest, I had missed her a little and she appeared now like a welcome old friend. On second thoughts, that is probably an exaggeration, but she was an ally against Roni – and in that direction I needed any help I could get. Anyway, the previous night Stella had been telling me that Iris would be disgusted at the way I had allowed myself to be used. 'You have to make a stand now', she had said vehemently. 'Make a stand now or you'll lose yourself forever'.

What had I got to lose?

'Are you fucking mad?' Roni's anger was almost palpable.

'Maybe I am – and whose fault is that?' My anger was building to match hers. 'Playing with my feelings, feeding me drugs to make me fall in love with you. What kind of monster uses—'

'Oh listen to yourself! I dragged you from obscurity and helped you find yourself!'

'Myself? You helped me find *myself*?' I spat the words out, proud that, with Stella's encouragement, I was finally standing up to her. 'I don't know who I am any more!'

'It's nerves.' She stood up and looked down at me pityingly. 'Jesus! It's like having to deal with my mother all over again!'

'Your mother? What the hell has she got to do with it?' She had succeeded in diverting my sense of purpose by arousing my curiosity. Roni never spoke about her dead mother and I never, perhaps instinctively, asked about her.

'*She* resisted my attempts to help her make something of herself too!' Her face was flushed and I'm sure I saw tears forming in her eyes. 'What the fuck did I do wrong?'

'You need to ask?' Stella was goading me again.

'I really can't believe your ingratitude.' She sighed loudly and looked up at the ceiling. Maybe she was trying to make the tears of frustration go back where they had come from. 'You've got the world at your feet because I've made it possible and now you haven't got the guts to see it through!'

'If possession of guts were the only requirement for fame and success, you'd have got there on your own!' I realized as the words came out that I might have hit the nail on the head a little too succinctly and touched a raw nerve. Stella knows a thing or two about striking below the belt.

'You're *worse* than my mother!' The tears were flowing freely now. 'Do you know what I'd give for the kind of talent she had – let alone what you've got?'

'What?' I was confused. 'You told me she wasn't a good actress.'

'She wasn't good at using what she had.' Her face hardened. 'She wasted her talent!' Without any further elucidation on the subject, I could see that she saw this as the worst sin in the world.

'Am I a replacement for her?' My confusion was growing, but it was tinged with sympathy and I wasn't sure why.

'What do you need from me? I mean it, Danny, tell me!' She looked me straight in the eye and spoke in a calm monotone. I thought this signalled the beginning of her surrender. Looking back now – and that of course depends on whether I am remembering the scene correctly – this sudden change of tack should have alerted me to the fact that she was plotting a new plan of attack. 'Tell me what you need!' Her tone became pleading.

'I need a replacement so I can have a night off! They'll understand. I mean, that's how I got my chance on "A Game of Two Halves". I'm not indispensible.'

'And you want to give some upstart a chance on the back of all the work I've done? Over my dead body!' With that, she jumped up – shooting me a murderous glance – and ran out of the door, taking the key with her. I heard it turn in the lock from the outside.

I was trapped in a dressing room, trapped in a marriage, trapped in a celebrity lifestyle. Stella asked me what Iris would think if she could see me locked in a room by a wife who had tricked me into loving her, so I told her to fuck off. She did and I was alone. Alone to ponder the look I had seen in Roni's eyes as she left; I had never seen such anger. I should have realized that she would stop at nothing if I defied her.

About half an hour later I heard a tap on the door followed by the key turning in the lock and jumped to my feet. 'Feeling any better darling?' Roni simpered as she put her head around the door. Her submissive, sympathetic performance as she came in told me that she wasn't alone. Sure enough, one of the assistant floor managers was hot on her heels carrying a tray of sandwiches and a carton of orange juice. 'I've got some aspirin to try to shift that headache. Thanks Darryl. Put it down on there please.' Her smile lasted until the door was closed and locked behind him. 'Right!' She turned to face me.

I honestly think I found out that night what it feels like to be trapped in a cage with a tiger. She sat down and pulled a small packet from her pocket. 'Bugger the aspirin! What you need is a nice big fat line of this! Now let me find my credit card.' As I watched in incredulous silence, she proceeded to expertly pour out a pile of white powder, chop it and form it into two lines on the dressing table in front of us. 'What are you waiting for?'

I'm not proud to admit it, but I was so genuinely afraid of her that I took the cocaine, snorting a line aggressively as if my life depended on it. Perhaps it did.

If you have ever experienced the effects of cocaine, you may identify with the fact that, initially, I wondered what all the fuss was about. I didn't feel any different. I didn't witness a sudden and overpowering sensation of euphoria. I certainly didn't feel that I was descending into the depths of wanton drug addiction. In retrospect, I don't think my experience was any different from most first time cocaine users.

But I did the television show.

Apparently – and I am basing this statement on the collective view of the critics – it was the best in the series so far.

The series progressed show by show, my performance lubricated by the initially small and later copious amounts of the drug I inhaled. Contrary to my first impression of its effects, I began to realize that they were liberating and – to a certain extent – enhancing. I began to believe in myself, but, at the same time, couldn't ignore the irony of the manufactured drug dependency story that had helped to launch me on the path on which I was now moving forward at an alarming speed. I even found myself ruminating on and even beginning to believe in the fact that there was a higher order involved and that this had all along been my destiny. I also cannot deny that my manner on screen had become more flamboyant and unguarded. But this is what happens when you allow self-belief to take hold.

'It's alright to be camp,' Roni was talking with her back to me as she got undressed, 'but don't let the viewers think you're gay.' We had just moved into a mews house in Pimlico – rented for the duration of the conversion of this Thames-side apartment in which I am now ensconced. Converted years earlier from the stables attached to a big Regency house, it had small cosy rooms furnished with ostentatiously large and expensive furniture. Overstuffed sofas, upholstered in piped damask, vied with reproduction Regency chests, sideboard and tallboy against a backdrop of swags and tails that closed in on the tiny living room. Huge gilt-framed prints of anatomically perfect horses and symmetrical country houses set in verdant gardens, some of which were duplicated in different rooms, lined the walls, giving me the feeling that I was a doll who had wandered into a dolls' house of the wrong size.

In Roni's view, it showed that we had made it. In mine, it smacked of the ridiculous: a former stable that looked as if it had been decorated by a Jewish pools winner. What did it matter, though? We would soon be moving to the riverside flat, the creation of which I was working hard at designing and overseeing.

Realizing that we could not only afford a building like this, but could also have a say in every detail of its conversion and construction had given me the boost I needed to justify my existence. From the moment we had spotted the opportunity one day when were having an apparently spontaneous lunch in a riverside pub (which I later found out had been cleverly engineered by Roni), I realized how much I needed a place of my own, a space I could design and organize, a space in which I could be myself. Now, when I was waiting for the start of each television show, I let myself escape mentally to this planned haven of peace and quiet, allowed myself to imagine the fabrics with which I would furnish it, let myself dream about the way the light would be diffused through those same fabrics and the resulting effects on the different, disparate materials I would bring together in the construction: new fruit wood, old oak, ancient flagstones, travertine marble, zelij tile and terracotta. For the first time in my life, I had become materialistic.

But it was materialism with a very particular purpose, I told myself: to provide room to escape from the life that so often threatened to crowd in on me. I would be able to look at the world without it looking back at me – a simple case of roles being reversed.

'Don't let the audience think you're gay,' she said. Her logic, combined with her ego, told her that if I didn't want her sexually, then I must be gay.

'Be yourself!'
'Be camp!'
'Don't act gay!'
'Sell yourself!'

I didn't know who the fuck I was, so how could I sell myself?

I stopped using cocaine immediately after I watched a recording of the fifteenth show in the series. I saw myself bringing an undeserving guest to tears live on air purely for the sake of comedy.

On most of our frequent visits to London's top restaurants, Roni used to delight in complaining. She pretended not to enjoy it and invariably preceded each complaint with something like 'I hate to complain but–' or 'You know I wouldn't complain unnecessarily but–', always accompanied with an apologetic expression. She saw it as getting what she was paying for, or what 'we' were paying for. Whether I liked it or not, we were a celebrity couple and Roni was intent on taking full advantage of the fact. I used to dread her ordering her fillet steak 'blue', knowing that she had no intention of eating it when it arrived. I have suspicions that she only ordered it in the first place because she knew it upset my vegetarian sensibilities.

Her favourite scenario involved a hapless waiter or waitress not understanding what she meant, which would then lead to a gentle, but nonetheless withering, explanation. The steak, when it came, would either be, in her estimation, not rare enough or, if it was, not of the quality suitable to be served so rare. She may have engineered my career, but she made her own out of complaining.

Stella – now a frequent visitor again – used to goad me to tell her what I thought. Phrases like 'spoilt cow', 'bloodsucking viper' and 'talentless frustrated bag' echoed in my head as Roni reduced yet another waiter to a quivering wreck, but then Stella was very rarely one to mince her words. I was never, in those days, brave enough to repeat them, but I occasionally managed eye contact with the waiter in question. It's amazing how far a surreptitious eye movement can go to restoring someone's confidence. It's that hazardous tennis-like game again. A little feedback and the energy is restored for another volley. The power is shifted and control is regained.

Nowadays I take an almost sadistic pleasure in cooking pieces of fillet steak until they are within a hair's breadth of being burnt. I let her tuna get too fishy by leaving it out in the kitchen all day and I have been known to cause myself to vomit when the temptation to sniff a plate of rancid prawns on their way to Roni has proved too much.
She used to complain, but she doesn't any more. The realization that, no matter how loud she shouts, no-one will hear may finally have dawned on her.

Tonight's letter – a beautiful 'A' – came from an early nineteenth century Jane Aitken's Bible I acquired from a dealer in the King's Road when ostensibly looking for light fittings for the guest suite. I have derived more pleasure from the Bible than I have from the light fittings I eventually found which came from Marrakech and were made by an artisan painstakingly cutting, beating and piercing metal teapots, then insetting them with blue stones. This doesn't imply that I made a poor choice with the light fittings, but that I have been unable to see them for nearly three years.

The Second TV Series

B

So, in accordance with Roni's plan, the following year saw my television show metamorphose into a five-nights-a-week phenomenon. Contrary to my expectations, the viewing public were genuinely delighted to lap up more of Danny Devereux's unique brand of entertainment. Obscene sums of money were quoted in the press and, to a certain extent, changed hands. I also had more of an input into the show's new format: it was shorter than the weekly show at forty minutes rather than an hour, with one guest rather than two and more room for improvisation with the audience. It goes without saying, of course, that any hints of my doing impressions or impersonations were stamped on immediately.

One day in a break in rehearsals I reduced the whole studio to fits of laughter with a quick vignette about Bette Davis and Tallulah Bankhead encountering a rattle snake whilst driving through the Arizona desert. Roni merely raised an eyebrow and shook her head. Once we were in the privacy of my dressing room, however, she turned on me, hands on hips and eyes flashing. 'You can't go back to that old crap now!' I could see tiny bits of spittle flying out of her mouth. 'For God's sake get it into your thick head that the public loves *you* not your fucking impressions! We've made it, so bloody well enjoy it!' It was an order that I was sadly incapable of obeying.

Stella had begun to tone down her approach on her now more frequent appearances. Maybe – well, almost definitely – she had come to the conclusion that a subtler mode of attack was more likely to make me listen to her. After all, my defences were constantly in place in order to survive life with Roni, so another source of stern admonition would only succeed in those defences being strengthened.

'You're limiting yourself,' she said gently one day, her voice almost unrecognizable for being pitched lower than normal with a genuine-sounding timbre of concern. 'She's scared of what you can do.' Strangely enough, I knew she was right. I also knew what was coming next. 'Just think how Iris encouraged you to develop your abilities.'

I silently thought that it wasn't only me she encouraged, but thought it best not to upset Stella's sense of self-worth when she was trying to be pleasant.

You may wonder how I came to agree to the second series. The answer is simpler than you might think.

Leading up to that time, I had felt trapped in a seemingly inescapable position – unable to return to what I used to be either physically or mentally. What, I had asked myself on many occasions, would I do with myself if I wasn't being propelled towards stardom by a wife who had taught me what it felt like to be in love?

This, however, had all changed with the acquisition of the buildings that were to become our new apartment (which I firmly saw as *my* apartment). I had found that there *was* something I could do. More than that, there was something at which I excelled. But just as I was getting used to this comforting and life-enhancing fact, it was very nearly snatched away from me by the harsh reality that our production company, the means by which we earned our living, was deeply in debt as a result of the expenditure on planning the second series. I had no choice.

Roni had made sure that I had no choice.

Looking on the bright side, the one good thing about the new series was that the set had curtains.

Across the Thames, right in my field of vision, are five enormous residential developments. Three are converted from old warehouses, one is made to look as if it was converted from one and the fifth is proudly new and industrial with sheets of plate glass supported and punctuated by steel girders, sheet zinc and black steel balconies. I sometimes wonder how many people live in them, then wonder further how many of them were enticed by the advertisements I have seen in the Evening Standard property supplement selling – or at least purporting to offer for sale – complete lifestyles rather than places in which to eat, wash and sleep. Does the reality ever live up to the dream promised?

In each development, the balconies are almost identical to each other, differing only in the splashes and dots of colour supplied by random pieces of outdoor furniture – rarely used for their intended purpose because of the virtually constant but unforeseen wind which blows almost relentlessly up and down the river – and struggling potted palms bought in optimistic moments by new owners still believing the brochures promising Mediterranean-style living flaunted by the developers. Such apartments, I fear, are more valuable as unachieved aspirations, which as such would never be revealed as falling short of their promises.

Unfulfilled dreams and unanswered prayers are undervalued commodities in this day and age. Being given choices, or at least being led to believe we have the power to choose how we live our lives, inevitably leads to disappointment and regret. Lack of choice, on the other hand, leaves no room for this eventuality and dreams are still intact.

Ironically, in the Sixties and Seventies council tenants were regularly moved from back-to-back terraced houses to high rise blocks similar to those on the other side of the river (albeit without the supposedly all-important river view) until it was widely recognized that such schemes were not only impractical, but also destructive to community, health and humanity. Just a few decades later, a different sector of society is being targeted to live this stacked-up existence and will – quite likely – follow the same route to become prisoners in their homes. In these cases it will be because their massive mortgages, which are meant to supply them with enriching and complete new lifestyles (as promised by the marketing material), render them hardly able to afford to go out.

Choices and regrets...

Watching these lives going on opposite me – or at least the settings for these lives – I realize that I find other people's lives interesting but not in the least appealing. I can't feel what they're feeling and I can only imagine what they're thinking.

Of course, when the television show went five nights a week, there was no question of me writing all my own material. I had at my disposal an excellent team of scriptwriters adept at emulating my 'inimitable style' as Roni put it (without a trace of intended irony).

'You can do it. Just be yourself.'

She implemented the buying of this place so that we could 'be ourselves'. In true Roni style, she acquired the different parts of the building from three separate owners. The result – following much planning, demolition and reconstruction – is unique. She said we needed complete privacy and individually designed luxury within easy reach of the studios on the South Bank.

The privacy nearly disappeared before we had even moved in: she organized no fewer than three magazine shoots and a slot on a celebrity lifestyle show – one in which a chummy presenter 'drops in' on famous people to see how and where they live, pretending that it's a natural and casual experience when reality dictates that designers and decorators have been ripping the place apart and putting it back together in television-friendly format for the preceding weeks. On one occasion I know of, a male pop star rented a breathtaking house in the country for the purpose and tried to pass it off as his own, but came unstuck because it belonged to a rather well known film actress who threatened to sue.

For once I had to take a deep breath and put my foot down, stating that if the apartment was thrown open to the gaze of the public in this way, I would have to fulfil my desire to buy a place in the countryside. I said I'd rather suffer the hassle of commuting every day than feel I was in the public eye even when at home.

'I know you would, darling,' she said, without an attempt at sincerity, 'but you must remember I've done all this for you.'

I know 'lost for words' wouldn't often be a state attributed to my public persona, but I quite often was when assaulted by Roni with such blatant assumptions of my gullibility. Did she really believe that I believed her? Or did she actually believe herself? The irony was, though, that the renovation of the apartment was giving me a new lease of life. I knew, without having to question why, that it would be to my advantage if she didn't know this.

The team of scriptwriters was consistently and satisfactorily productive, then systematically fired and replaced as a symptom of Roni's need to feel creatively involved. Our researchers proved to be worth their weight in gold, available studio seats were as rare as hen's teeth and the ratings soared.

Roni was in her element.

I was absolutely exhausted.

The upside of it was that, before the second series began, I had categorically stated that it would be my last. In fact, it had been a condition of my signing the contract. I know this may sound as if I was being something of a prima donna, but I was genuinely concerned about my ability to carry on. I wouldn't have wanted to sign up for something that I wasn't able to see through to fruition.

There were ninety shows in the series and, from the first one, I used to count how many were left until the end. Standing behind the curtains – which at least I had now so the fear and nausea could be contained behind their physical boundaries – I could see the shows stretching out ahead of me. Coming back through the curtains at the end of each show, I used to imagine another scratch on the imaginary brick wall. Every show was one step nearer to being able to stop, one step nearer to having a rest. In retrospect it seems laughable, but I actually thought that by doing this I was gaining some control over my life.

Knowing that I had set a limit to the number of performances I was to give endowed me with the impetus to put more into each and every one of them. I realize now that I was naïve to think that Roni would ever let me stop.

I took to the role of liaising between architects, builders, plumbers and electricians like the proverbial duck to water. This, I realized with relief, was what I would do when I retired from live television. It was the first occupation in which I could imagine myself to be, if not happy, at least content. I just knew I would be able to identify the exact nature of the living space my prospective clients needed even if they didn't themselves. I would be meeting a demand and serving a practical purpose by converting dreams into reality.

I haven't yet got my outfit ready for tonight's Night Delivery because my day was thrown into slight disarray earlier when my cleaning routine was interrupted by a loud clattering which sounded as if it was coming from the guest suite. I obviously dropped everything and rushed up there, only to discover the noise wasn't coming from there at all. I looked carefully out of the kitchen window and found that it was caused by a team of workmen on a truck outside mending the streetlights. But by that time my routine had been interrupted and I had to start all over again.

My need for order doesn't completely rule my life, but it could if I let it. Usually I can tell when one of my particularly dark moods is coming and nip it in the bud before it drags me down, making life seem futile, pointless and without aim. Ironically, it's this tendency

I am saddled with that gives me the potential for creativity. Coupled as it is with an inherent streak of self-loathing, it apparently makes me destined to either succeed or fail in a spectacular fashion.

Without it, I wouldn't be where I am today. Instead, I would likely be in some comfortable job either in search of or enjoying contentment.

With it, I am in constant danger of self-destruction.

So I can sympathize entirely with these men who have chosen to die. For what are they dying? For whom are they dying? Quite simply, they are dying for money, which I suppose is quite a lot less futile than randomly committing suicide. Is a life ended prematurely for this reason any less worthwhile than a long, useless existence?

I'm not asking you, by the way. I'm asking myself.

The Argument

E

The countdown to the end of the series was underway. My anticipation of having some time to myself while I planned my new career was growing daily. So to say that the news that Roni was negotiating terms for another series came as a shock to me would be a serious understatement. As if this wasn't enough, this news was followed by the revelation that she was also working on the format for yet another show.

'What the hell do you think you're playing at?' I burst into the study in which she spent most of the time when we were at home in the Pimlico mews house. My anger went some of the way to help me control my fear; I felt like an animal which had just realized that it was in a cage from which it would never escape. 'How can you make plans like this without even consulting me?'

'I think your reaction is supplying the answer to that question, darling,' she said in a calm, condescending manner without looking away from the computer screen.

'So you don't think I need to have a say in the matter?' I can't remember whether anger or fear was foremost in my mind at the moment I said those words, but both sentiments were definitely there. Even though I was under no illusions about the amount of hard work and determination Roni had put into the company, there was no getting away from the fact that I was its chief asset. The problem was, though, that I wasn't really the commodity being marketed and sold; it was this other 'me' Roni had coerced into existence and the strain of 'being myself' all the time was becoming increasingly intolerable. The only thing that had been keeping me going was the knowledge that it would soon come to an end. And that knowledge, and the hope that came with it, was slipping away from my grasp.

'Danron's new project,' Roni told me calmly in a tone of voice normally reserved by a parent for a recalcitrant child, 'is taking tactical advantage of the phenomenal success of our television show.' She still didn't look up from her computer. 'Who would have thought ratings would remain so high with the show running five times a week?' She sounded almost detached. If she was trying to give me the impression that she wasn't taking me seriously, she was succeeding. 'So you can't deny, darling, that I've got our best interests at heart, can you?' The question was accompanied by a tinkling, apparently light-hearted laugh. Its steely undertone sent a chill running through me. 'How could we,' she paused for emphasis, 'be *stupid* enough to miss out on the opportunities now open to us?'

Just before The Shooting, our net worth was purported to be in excess of seven million pounds.

My protestations that the first television series was meant to be a testing ground after which I was to be allowed to decide how much further my television career went, not to mention the fact that the five nights a week show had been very much against my better judgment, seemed to fall on deaf ears.
'You got your bloody curtains didn't you?'
'Yes.' I couldn't deny it. They were massive purple velvet ones suspended from a gold proscenium arch through which I bounded – or should I say 'I' bounded – at the beginning of each show.
'So what the fuck are you complaining about?'
I was a commodity and a valuable one at that, but worth nothing if I wasn't kept in control. I thought that knowing this gave me power.

Just before The Argument, the Friends got together at the mews house while I was busy at the still unfinished new apartment and estimated that Danron Productions' net worth – even allowing for the New Show being only moderately successful – could have doubled within the next twelve months to fourteen million. I wasn't consulted or involved.

I always start the daily cleaning in the main living area, first drawing back the massive swathes of grey muslin edged with orange and gold braid imported specially from India and opening the windows to let in a breeze from the river which, I have to admit, is not always as fresh as it could be. The floors are mostly the wooden ones original to the building, sanded and polished but retaining a pleasing patina hinting at their years of use, so cleaning them – with the help of a large industrial vacuum cleaner – is a positive joy. I push back the furniture – three large chesterfields upholstered in soft grey leather and a large wooden chest, which started off its life as a magician's transfer trunk – onto the limestone floor in the dining area, above which a huge oak door serving as a dining table is suspended on heavy cables. I then work across the floor methodically. The ergonomically designed head of the vacuum cleaner is slightly wider than the boards, so there is very little danger of missing any dust.

I start against the exposed brick wall, which still bears the marks of the building's former incarnation as a meat warehouse – steel straps bolted along the wall once supported racks of hooks for carcasses – and work my way across to the windows overlooking the river then, to make sure, work my way back again. I follow this with a light mopping with a very mild detergent solution, working from the meat wall to the window wall, then, while the floor is drying, I clean the insides of the windows with damp newspaper, then let the curtains back down to billow in the breeze. Moving the sofas and chest back to the middle of the room accounts for some of my daily exercise; physical exertion, I have realized for many years, is as important as its mental counterpart.

Next I turn my attention to the dining area and adjoining kitchen. The limestone floor is not original to the building. It apparently came from a quarry in Jerusalem. I am willing to believe it, but unlikely to be ever able to prove it. Belief is, as I have said before, the backbone of existence. This part of the apartment was originally a shop – most recently selling wholesale cosmetics – before we bought it along with the meat warehouse and gaslight importer's storeroom, which had been disused for more than forty years. How typical of Roni to be able to negotiate the purchase of three derelict properties and, by facilitating the removal and replacement of walls, raising and lowering of floors, erecting of staircases and moving of windows – which entailed seemingly endless arguments with the planning authority – enable the creation of a stunning and individual home.

It really could have been featured in the magazines Roni was so keen to allow to invade our privacy. I can almost imagine them fawning at its 'wow factor'. Massive oak beams over-slung with hemp ropes supporting two illuminated bicycles ('a humorous departure from the everyday chandelier' I can hear them saying) are offset by what appears to be literally acres of fabric in a rainbow of hues and textures from all over the world (all chosen by me, I hasten to add). Old contrasts with new, functional sits with purely decorative, industrial blends with domestic and, above all, the whole comes together as a stunning home which, strangely, doesn't seem at all contrived. I like to think it's the knack which would have given me a satisfying career if I'd had the chance to put it to the test.

And now Roni and I live in it. But not together. And certainly not happily.

Cleaning the kitchen takes a maximum of forty seven minutes, allowing ten minutes to buff up all the stainless steel surfaces with a soft cloth and hint of baby oil. I pull up the stainless steel Venetian blinds one at time and clean the windows behind them, being careful to duck down if there is anyone outside in the street. For the blinds themselves I have a special cleaning tool – like a squeegee with a slit in it – with which I can clean all three in five minutes. I like to stand back for a moment at this point and survey my gleaming handiwork.

While I chose, designed and sourced virtually all the fixtures, fittings, furniture and furnishings in the place, Roni insisted on the solid, stainless steel extra-durable industrial kitchen in preparation for, and anticipation of, the massive celebrity-strewn dinner parties we were seemingly destined to host around the oak door dining table rescued from a Maltese convent ('rescued' being a slight euphemism, since it was torn from its original setting and sold to us at great expense by an international architectural salvage merchant).

Needless to say, there has never been a dinner party here because The Shooting brought an abrupt end to our celebrity lifestyle. Or at least it appeared to. I had, of course, sounded the death knell on it already.

Leading down from the main living area is a flight of stone stairs which end at a pair of heavy iron-clad doors that open directly onto the river just above the high-water level. Roni's intention was to buy a motor launch in which we could zoom back and forth to the studio: yet another unfulfilled dream. A similar flight of stairs leads up to what was designed as the guest bedroom suite. The heavy oak door at the top of the stairs, complete with its original cast iron hinges and bolts, leads to an inner foyer – 'for complete privacy' the architect told us – which in turn leads to the suite itself, which used to be the manager's office. The old safe set into the wall is one of the original features I incorporated into the design, along with a small goods lift with exquisite mahogany sliding casement doors and three tall windows with heavy steel bars on the inside overlooking what is now the main living area. The manager obviously needed to feel secure, while at the same time being able to see that his workers weren't slacking without having to smell them or the bloodied carcasses they handled.

Guests have never stayed in the guest suite. I don't clean it for obvious reasons.

I turn my hand to cleaning the study next, which takes four and a half minutes, then move on to Roni's dressing room next door, which takes about the same time. Both of these rooms have no windows, don't gather dust and don't need much cleaning, but I still prefer to do them every day. If I stopped this daily routine, how would I decide on which days it should or shouldn't be done? I open the wardrobes to let air circulate through the rows and rows of Roni's clothes hanging there. They are all clothes that, with the exception of one outfit, she will quite possibly never wear again. I close the wardrobe again and move on to the main bedroom. My bedroom.

Reached by a kind of glass and steel drawbridge leading up through an arched opening punched into the sturdy brick wall of the old meat warehouse, my bedroom occupies the space that used to be the gas lamp storeroom. Heavy interlined curtains fronted with grey muslin edged with orange and gold braid to match the others in the main living space hang in the doorway. I like the sensation that comes with parting the weighty conglomeration of fabric and stepping into my bedroom, the space exclusively dedicated to – and occupied by – me.

From inside, the curtains are lined with iridescent purple watered silk. It took more than seventy metres of this fabric, apparently still produced and woven in Aleppo using the process formulated by the Phoenicians, to decorate the room. The Georgian four poster bed, the arched windows with their river view and the opening to the walk-in wardrobe are all hung with expertly tailored curtains in the same fabric, which reflects the light differently according to the time of day. Now, it being morning, the curtains have a brighter, pinkish sheen which gives the room a blushing glow as I strip the crisp white Egyptian cotton sheets from the bed.

The crucifix above the headboard, which isn't as heavy as it looks, lifts down easily and I lay it across the bed, to be joined by a large bronze Ganesha, a Jewish menorah from the windowsill, the Buddha from the floor beside the bed, an almost life-size statue of the Virgin Mary, a prayer mat from the floor at the foot of the bed, a silver chalice, an icon of the Archangel Michael and a statue of Shiva from the ledge beside the bathroom alcove. Then I fetch the small vacuum cleaner from the wardrobe and, with a soft brush attachment, dust all the walls, shelves and windowsills, then change the attachment and clean the black and white chequered floor, one tile at a time. The windows, being small, take only two minutes to clean and the plain white bathroom seven and a half. Including the time taken to replace everything and put clean sheets on the bed, cleaning my bedroom takes no more than twenty seven minutes.

The proposed show, or 'New Show' as Roni was already calling it, sounded completely ridiculous to me. But the proposal to do a show five nights a week had also seemed ludicrous to me at the proposal stage. It was to run concurrently with the next series, the existence of which was already being taken for granted even though I was steadfastly refusing to sign a contract. I had kept my side of the bargain, I said, and now needed a rest.

I at last knew what I wanted to do with my life. My vocation would be to create functional, beautiful and life-enhancing homes. But first I needed to get away from my public persona for a while to formulate my future. The seeds I had planted in my own mind needed to germinate, take root and become established. No matter how many times, how quietly or loudly I repeated these sentiments, Roni either couldn't or wouldn't understand. Rather than putting her energies into persuading me to sign for the next series, despite the fact that nothing she could have said or done would have swayed my mind, she was leaping ahead to this 'New Show' which would run on Saturdays in the early evening. I couldn't believe that the viewing public, having seen or had the opportunity to see me five times a week already, would possibly want to stomach any more. 'Different Format', 'New Audience' and 'Fresh Market' were labels bandied around. But I was resolute. For once, I was not going to be coerced into something I didn't want to do.

Roni finally realized I was serious when The Argument came to a head.

I suppose I had better describe the proposed format of the 'New Show' in order for you to understand why I behaved the way I did. It was entirely Roni's brainchild, to give her credit where it is due, and at first I thought she had put together the proposal purely to annoy me. Before long, however, I realized she was deadly serious about it. I can see now – with the benefit of hindsight – that Roni was ahead of the competition in her thinking. Her brainchild would quite probably have been an unmitigated success.

It was to be a talent show, for want of a more specific category, in which I would seek out gifted amateurs. 'Natural Talent', another of Roni's new labels, was apparently in plentiful supply and who better than me to go and mix with the unwashed masses and sort the wheat from the chaff?

'More than seventy per cent of the population wants fame,' she said as if she was an authority on the subject, 'so why not give them the chance to prove whether or not they've got the talent to warrant it?'

'So the fact that it would be incredibly cheap television to make is not the main factor then?' I asked earnestly.

'It's naturally a factor, but not the main one.' She shook her head at me conveying a mixture of disappointment and bewilderment. 'I'm doing it for us. We,' she said (emphasizing the 'we' as usual), 'are the perfect team to do it.' She omitted any mention or discussion of the facts that, by contractually tying up any real talent discovered, Danron Productions could only be set to profit. 'We'll be giving something back to our public.' This feigned discovery of a philanthropic streak caused me to laugh loudly and openly. She gave me a dark look combining confusion and pitying worldliness.

And that was before she dropped the bombshell that she intended to co-host the show. Veronica Bedford: self-styled talent guru, discoverer and developer of raw talent, saviour of the talented but fameless. She was furious at my derision, or perhaps at my lack of attempt to hide it, but nothing like as furious as she was when I categorically refused to have anything to do with it.

Roni employed various tactics, the most notable and unusual of which was complete silence, to attempt to make me come around to her way of thinking. When these failed, she opted for giving me what she saw as terrifying glimpses of what life would be like without success, success to her being synonymous with fame and celebrity status.

'Do you honestly want an anonymous existence away from the public eye?' It was clearly intended as a rhetorical question, but proved how little she knew about my aims and desires.

She used the words 'aimless', 'futile' and 'pointless' rather too often, which served only to bolster my occasionally flagging determination. I could see her working herself up into an ever-increasing frenzy at being out of control.

'You're not even *trying* to see it from my point of view,' she said one day, quietly. 'I don't know what to say that can change your mind.'

'I know,' I said with relief.

'You're fucking impossible!' Her tone was no longer quiet, her patience running out, her need for control compromised.

I can't deny that I found it pleasing and, the more I saw that she was losing her control over me, the more I rose to meet the challenge. Then Stella stepped in. And The Argument came to a head.

It was unfortunate that Stella decided to become vocal at the point that Roni was finally coming around to the idea of me having a month off 'to decide on the future'. But that's Stella. I suppose she'd been cooped up inside me for too long. She caught me off guard and managed – for the first time – to have her say in Roni's presence. But I'll tell you about that later.

Our social life, which was entirely engineered by Roni since I neither wanted nor had one of my own, was populated by her Friends, with whom she declared she could 'be herself' – a luxury of which I didn't even let myself dare to dream. Even when she said, more than once, that my job was easy compared to hers, I managed to force myself to refrain from saying anything. Until, that is, one of her seemingly flippant insults pushed me over the edge.

I had merely refused to come downstairs for a lunch party with her Friends, an invasion she had sprung on me with only an hour's notice, which proved in itself that she knew I wouldn't like it. It was Sunday – a cherished day of rest. 'Please, Roni, I need to lie down quietly and collect myself for the week ahead.'

Looking back, I can see that I was more exhausted than usual and she was still recovering from her monthly tribulation. As usual, she had been completely incapacitated with excruciating pain that invariably left her with no choice but to take to her bed. There were times when my heart went out to her: a control freak relinquishing her power to the greater powers – limiting powers – of nature. These harsh monthly reminders of her gender served to highlight her basic inability to reproduce, underlining her barrenness with white hot shards of ironic pain. I had, as usual, done my best to be sympathetic, but now needed time alone.

'For God's sake, Danny!' She stood over me as I reclined on the bed. 'After all I've done for you, you can't even be bothered to get your sorry arse downstairs to be sociable.' I was trying hard not to listen until she spat out the next scorn-laden words. 'You're such a fucking drama queen!'

I'm still not sure why this particular barbed comment was the one that inspired the events that followed. I certainly hadn't been planning to do what I did.

Roni slammed the bedroom door behind her and went downstairs to make sure the caterers were doing as she had asked. Without any warning at all, Stella suddenly perked up.

'I've told you before, it's because she's scared of what you can do.'

'So?' I wasn't in the mood for Stella either.

'Maybe it's a good time to show her.' There was an unmistakable wickedness in her tone. 'Or at least it will be when the audience arrives.'

An hour later, I went downstairs and wandered into the kitchen where Roni was quietly but firmly instructing a small Malaysian girl to change the prawns adorning the salad for larger ones. She looked up and smiled. There was an distinctive look of relief on her face. 'I'm glad you've got over your little sulk, darling.' She kissed me, unable to hide a satisfied smirk as she handed me a large gin and tonic. 'Now go into the drawing room and entertain our friends.' The Friends were not my friends. But I was sure as hell going to entertain them.

Less than five minutes later, Roni came hurriedly into the room to discover the source of the merriment. Ellie's raucous laughter had obviously travelled down the long corridor to the kitchen. The smile that was on Roni's face as she entered – probably thinking that I had at last decided that obeying her orders was the best way forward – was soon replaced by a look of horrified disbelief, which in turn gave way to a malevolent scowl.

'Oh Roni!' Ellie could barely speak for laughing as she used her silk scarf to wipe her eyes, careless of the effect on her eye make-up. 'He's... he's... well, darling, he's more *you* than *you* are!'

Hadn't she told me to entertain them? I'd started the impression out in the hall before I entered the room. They were all obviously used to listening to Roni, but I don't think I'm flattering myself when I say that I had all three of them fooled until I actually walked into the room. Once I realized I'd got their attention, I moved on to doing Roni doing a Norma Desmond type monologue about the New Show.

'I *hate* that word! It's a *return!*'

I had never impersonated Roni before, but it came more easily than it perhaps should have. Ellie's raucous cackling told me I had hit the spot. There was clearly nothing this pack of Friends liked more than laughing at the expense of one of their own.

I was nearing the end of the impromptu performance when Roni walked in. And, to my credit, I stuck to my guns and finished it despite a venomous glare clearly designed to silence me.

I didn't have lunch with them.

We did the five shows that week without exchanging a single word. I thought Roni might have learned from her mistake of calling me a drama queen. But it didn't stop her forcing Stella to say what she did five days later. Of course, I'm not denying total responsibility but, in my defence, I had just finished the fifth show of the week and was exhausted – too tired to be able to control Stella when she decided suddenly to appear and tell Roni exactly what she thought of her.

'Would you really rather be traipsing around the circuit with your wigs and pigeons doing tawdry impersonations in sleazy dives wearing costumes made from old curtains?' It wasn't the first time Roni had dropped scorn on my early career. She had a look on her face that told me she was intent on causing not just offence but real hurt, but I don't honestly think her words bothered me. 'Maybe you need to actually face the fact that without me you'd be nothing!' Never feeling the need to refute her claims, I was well beyond being offended by most of the things she could come out with and would have been quite content to say nothing. Stella, on the other hand, could contain herself no longer and literally put words into my mouth.

'Nothing without you?' Stella paused, but I knew it was for dramatic effect, rather than that she hadn't got anything else to say. I was right. 'And where exactly would you be without Danny, you talentless has-been?' Her tone remained calm to heighten the cutting truth the words conveyed. 'Actually, you're not even a has-been – you're a never-was!' I can remember Roni's mouth falling open in stunned silence as Stella egged me on to take up where she had left off.

'You're a joke!' The words were my own now. 'Thinking up a new show you can co-host just to get some of that limelight you've been craving all these years. You're a joke – a pathetic joke!' There was still no utterance from Roni's open mouth. 'I don't have to ask you if I want to take a month off! I don't even have to consult you if I decide never to work again!'

That stung, I could tell. The possibility of my never working again was clearly a more unthinkably disastrous outcome than she could have allowed herself to imagine. Like the dangerous game I played every time I went before an audience, the volley had been started. My words had got a reaction, which fed their source and opened the floodgates.

When I was cleaning the study this morning, I had the sudden and uncharacteristic urge to look at the script for my last ever television show. This then resulted – perhaps inevitably – in having to get out all the scripts for the second series and lay them out, side by side, in chronological order. I was left wondering whether – during the course of the series – Danny Devereux became more like me or I became more like him.

'In fact,' I continued, 'since you seem to have neither idea of nor regard for my feelings and desires, it may be better if we decide to go our separate ways.'

'Danny.' Roni's face seemed to have been drained of all colour. 'You can't possibly mean that!'

'No?' This was the first time in years I had managed to make her listen to me and I wasn't going to waste the opportunity. 'How would you know what I mean? How would you know what I want?' I paused, counting the beats in my head. 'How would you know what I *feel*?'

'But,' there were tears in her eyes, 'I thought we had an understanding.'

'Understanding?' I laughed (or quite possibly 'I' laughed). 'Since when have you even asked me what I wanted? How could we have an understanding, Roni?'

'I'm at a loss for what to say.' She rummaged in her handbag for a tissue and dabbed at her eyes. 'I've always pushed you towards goals and you've always responded by achieving them.'

'But always on *your* terms!' I wasn't being fooled by her tears.

'*My* terms?' Her tone hardened. 'You ungrateful little shit!' Strangely, I felt more at ease as the old vindictive Roni returned. 'You're like my bloody mother!' I'd heard this before. 'How will you be able to live with yourself if you waste your talent? You might as well kill yourself like she did!' Her eyes flashed with hatred. 'Let me know if you need a hand!' I had a sudden but unpleasant image of her mother's demise, but put it down to my overactive imagination. 'If you throw away what we've got together, you'll live to regret it!' Unfortunately, I didn't take her words as seriously as I should have.

I'm the first to admit that too much talent can be as much of a curse as none at all, but the possession of too much talent wasn't Roni's problem. While she was by no means without any, she wasn't in possession of a surfeit. To this day, if we were in a position to discuss it, she would no doubt insist that she was a victim of circumstance. She was, but not in the way she would like to think. To put it simply, an imbalance of ambition and talent can cause great unhappiness. It has for both of us.

I have been entertained by the disparate theories surfacing in the broadcast media regarding the tattooed corpses in the Thames. Nobody has come near to identifying the true story. Or, for that matter, the intended one.

I am ready early for this Night Delivery, so have decided to do my own tattoo first instead of afterwards. I am getting to quite enjoy the strange, tickling pain of the electric needle as it describes the letter, ingratiating the ink indelibly into the skin of my forearm.

The Shooting

D

The Shooting occurred two years, three hundred and fifty-three days ago at a villa on a previously little-known Greek island in the Ionian Sea. I imagine that you are no stranger to the fact, since the story was well documented at the time. What you will have seen was, however, only the apparent story.

Things calmed down a bit in the weeks following The Argument, Roni choosing to avoid the issue rather than to prolong hostilities. I suppose this should have alarmed me, but I suppose I thought she was finally taking me seriously. Fortunately, most of my time away from the television studios was spent overseeing the finishing touches being put to the apartment, a creative pastime that consumed me with an unconditional passion that I knew wouldn't be put to the test by an audience – unless, of course, I counted the numerous dinner guests Roni intended to invite, which I didn't.

I had stuck to my guns over taking a month's holiday on my own to 'recuperate' – the use of the word implying that it was me who had a problem. The truth of the matter was that I didn't see it as a month off as such, but as a chance to make a clean break and gather my thoughts in preparation for whatever steps I needed to take to embark on the next chapter of my life. I had little doubt that Roni would have a much smaller role to play in its next phase. In true Roni style, she made out that this sabbatical was completely her idea and set about recommending suitable destinations. The long and the short of it was that she decided that I would spend the month in an exclusive hotel created from a palazzo in the Tuscan countryside. I was to leave London the day after the last show of the series aired.

'I know you'll be happy with your choice,' she gushed as we supervised our belongings going into boxes and crates around us. I got the distinct impression that she was talking for the benefit of the removal men rather than to me. 'Rex always sends his clients there when they need to get away from the public eye. You'll have a private telephone in your suite, so there's no need to feel isolated.' Roni couldn't bear not knowing where I was and what I was doing at all times. 'You'll come back feeling like a new man!'

Looking back now, it seems rather absurd that I could have even entertained the notion that things would work out – that I would go away for a month, then come back to persuade Roni that I had had enough of my television career and was going to pursue a change of direction. Positive thoughts like this one were all I had to keep me going through the long and disordered days when I felt my life was out of control.

Will I look back at what I am doing now and think the same?

'So now this is home!' I punched in the alarm code we had agreed upon and closed the door behind us, doing my best to sound cheerful and upbeat. It was the night of the last television show and, although my exhaustion was threatening to get the better of me, I was determined not to allow our first night in the new apartment to be an anti-climax. Unable to ignore the irony that I was counting the minutes until my escape the next day, I looked to Roni for her reaction to our new living space.

'Don't go!' It wasn't the reaction I was expecting. I had a rare glimpse of her vulnerability and saw it as a sign of her feeling that she was losing control. 'I need you! You're the creative one and I'm just your infertile manager.' Her time of the month was just passing again and her words caused an involuntary lump to form in my throat as she reached for my hand, a forlorn figure seemingly lost in this vast apartment I had designed and brought to completion. 'Please come and sleep with me tonight.' Although we had been sleeping in separate rooms for months by then, I let her take my hand, let her put it gently to her face as the tears began to flow. 'I'm sorry Danny.'

'It's only a month,' I whispered, desperately wanting her not to plead with me. I hastily walked to the kitchen and found the bottle of Dom Perignon that I knew was waiting for us in the fridge. 'Can you find a couple of glasses?' She obediently rummaged around in a box and found some crystal flutes which had been purchased in more optimistic times.

I couldn't, I told myself as I eased the cork out and heard the satisfying pop it made, deny myself this recuperative time away for which I had struggled long and hard. Part of me knew that I had to get away from my wife in order to be able to think clearly. But another part of me had a brief glimpse of a future with Roni still being possible.

'We can make it work can't we?' The fact that she had framed it as a question rather than a statement or – as was more usual – a command, gave me hope that an amicable conclusion to our predicament was possible.

'I'm sure we can.' I poured the effervescent liquid into the glasses she was holding. She put one in my outstretched hand.

'To us!' Her attempt at forced enthusiasm brought a lump to my throat. She no longer scared me because she no longer seemed to be in control. We drank this sombre toast to a partnership that was suddenly back on even terms. What I needed to do, I decided, was to stop fighting against her. She was, I told myself, only a human being with her own unique feelings and vulnerabilities. If I could overcome my resentment to what she had done in the past, she would respond favourably and we would be able to work out terms for a future together.

The champagne brought with it a wave of buoyant confidence. A benevolent voice in my head told me that I had been at fault and that my own fear and insecurity had led her to behave as she did. It was the same voice that told me not to resist when she led me to the guest suite that night. My desire for everything to be calm, for the fighting to stop and for life to carry on without battles overrode an inner sense of foreboding that, even in rekindling our sex life, Roni had an ulterior motive.

'You're hurting me!' Roni's sudden exclamation stopped me in mid thrust and made me withdraw in dismay. My compassionate optimism evaporated. Even in this most intimate of acts she had to be in control. With a wink that made me shudder, she expertly brought me to a climax, then disappeared swiftly to the bathroom. I lay uneasily on the carefully-chosen Egyptian cotton sheets, thankful that I was escaping the next day.

The next morning dawned and, with a reasonably clear head, I kissed Roni goodbye and got into the car that had arrived to take me to Heathrow airport. As the journey progressed, London – although it was the same city it had been the day before – revealed itself as a more optimistic place. As I passed cars of all makes and colours, shops, schools, restaurants, trees and houses, I saw them all in a new light and caught glimpses of the people whose individual lives went on day by day in the bustling capital city. My spirits had been lifted because I was going abroad and was going to be allowed to be by myself – something I had rarely been able to do since I had met my wife.

The driver pulled up at the airport and summoned a porter to carry my luggage. An airline representative was waiting for me and I was helped to check in and sent on my way through security. It did occur to me at that point that it was curious that celebrities who, for the most part, are successful because of their own abilities are treated like incompetent children as a result. Or was I missing the element of enjoyment in this kind of treatment? I certainly wouldn't miss it when it was no longer on offer.

As I sat in the airport lounge waiting for my flight to Florence, I couldn't help feeling slightly smug at having been able to make alternative travel plans without Roni finding out. Little did I know what the consequences of those plans would be.

I was in Italy for a little more than an hour. My flight there had been excellent, but then first class flights should be. The British flight attendants had clearly recognized me but, in their obsequiously aloof manner, had made a very good job of pretending that either they didn't or that they thought celebrity status was nothing to be proud of. Collecting my luggage and skilfully avoiding the driver sent to meet me at the airport, I checked in for and boarded a charter flight – booked on the internet – to a small airport on mainland Greece. It amused me that the luxurious suite at the Italian palazzo would stand empty for a month with its private telephone line unused.

Squashed into a window seat beside a large Italian woman who insisted on doing everything for her adjacent son, including fastening his seat belt and taking the foil off his meal for him, I felt an intoxicating rush of anonymity. Nobody on the whole plane knew who I was. But then again, nobody in the country where I performed live on television five nights a week knew who I was either. Not who I really was.

Watching the mother next to me fussing over her son, who was, incidentally, in his mid twenties and had clearly never been allowed to cope without her, made me wonder what would have happened if Roni hadn't come into my life. But such ruminations were pointless at that stage. I drew the stiff plastic blind down on the window, sat back in the seat and closed my eyes feeling safe in the knowledge that no-one on that aeroplane was expecting anything from me.

The plane touched down on a small dusty runway and, after a round of applause – as if the passengers hadn't really expected it to land safely – and a lot of animated and vocal jostling when the seat belt lights went off, it was ascertained that we were to leave the aircraft by the rear door. I remained in my seat and chuckled to myself at the quantity of words needed to express even a simple desire in Italian. The mother and son exchanged something in the region of four hundred and fifty in order to arrive at the decision that he would retrieve her large fake Louis Vuitton handbag from the overhead locker for her. It reminded me of an old altercation between Joan Collins and Sophia Loren back in the Early Days inspired by a full-length fur Iris had been keeping in one of her wardrobes for more than twenty years.

The heat hit me as I wandered down the steps and onto the tarmac. A few people just outside the airport building were hastily smoking cigarettes and, even though I hadn't smoked in years, I had a sudden urge to join them. A man in a sharply cut suit, looking completely out of place amidst the Greek chaos, offered me a Marlboro Light, which I took gratefully, followed by his proffered lighter. How long had it been it since I'd bummed a cigarette? The sensation it gave me, which had little to do with nicotine, told me it was too long.

The real lift to my spirits came when I walked through passport control and the immigration officer gave my passport, which obviously bore my real name rather than my celebrity name, no more than a cursory glance. I was free for a whole month! I felt as if I was walking on air as I pushed through the crowd to grab my luggage from the jerkily progressing carousel and proceeded into the rudimentary arrivals hall.

A large unshaven man wearing a Manchester United football shirt was bearing a card with 'Ruddock' scrawled on it. I put up a hand and smiled, glad to be Daniel Ruddock again, even though I was and still am the first to admit that Ruddock was never a suitable name for a television personality. He grabbed my hand and shook it warmly. 'Welcome to Greece Mr Ruddock!' I matched his smile with my own and followed him to a battered Mercedes. His refreshingly unselfconscious monologue included football, Madonna and the state of British monarchy as he drove me out of the shabby airport, through some delightful villages that were refreshingly devoid of the concrete stamp left by package holiday companies on sunny island communities. We crossed a floating bridge connecting the mainland to a large island, then he dropped me at a bustling quayside, where I was to wait a little over half an hour for a ferry to my destination.

This felt like the backpacking I'd never done in my teens and I wished I'd found a way to swap my suddenly smart-looking suitcase for a battered rucksack. It crossed my mind to throw it into the sea and buy a pair of shorts and T-shirt from one of the shops by the quay. The wonderful truth was that I could have done so if I had wanted to. I really was free at last! I was at liberty to be myself, or at least to embark on a voyage of self-discovery, on an island largely undiscovered by mainstream tourists.

The ferry clanked into port with its ramp already down and disgorged a motley array of vehicles, people and animals. I was caught up in the rush to get on board, securing a place for myself and my suitcase up at the front. As the rusting vessel, named 'Freedom', pulled out to sea, a dolphin jumped up out of the water and played on the bow for a few moments. I saw it as a message. Little did I know that it was a portent of doom telling me to enjoy the moment, however fleeting, for what it was.

I was the only tourist alighting at my destination – the ferry's third stop. Three burly locals in a pick-up piled high with watermelons and an elderly couple on a moped, the wrinkled, walnut brown lady riding side saddle on the back, trundled off ahead of me, leaving me to attract the attention of the only taxi on the island, which was fortunately waiting nearby. I showed the driver the address of the villa, he nodded knowingly, lifted my suitcase into his boot and opened one of the rear doors for me. The interior of the car was filthy, its torn flannelette seat covers emitting a canine odour, but I was happier than if I'd been in the back of a vintage Rolls Royce being served Cristal champagne by Claudia Schiffer.

As we set off on our rattling journey, the taxi driver eagerly told me that, although very few tourists visited the island, its inhabitants were all doing their best to rectify that. There was no crime on the island, he said, if you didn't include a drunk Albanian trying to ride a donkey without the permission of its owner three weeks earlier, and the local olives were the best this side of the Peloponnese. I could sense a mixture of pride in his place of birth and frustration that it hadn't yet been discovered.

I wanted to extol the value of anonymity to him, but realized the incongruity of doing so. Who was I to patronize him? It's too easy to deride something you have in praise for something you've lost to someone who hasn't yet tasted it. Here was a man simply trying to make a living, whereas I was finding fault with a career beyond most people's wildest dreams. I felt myself sinking into a state of ruminative despair, until the driver pointed at a white painted villa on a steep hillside above us. It was my villa.

The cloud lifted and I could see clearly. At last I could be myself. I was to spend a whole month here alone – a whole month without anyone, particularly Roni, knowing where I was. I had a sudden and overwhelming sense of deja-vu and knew that this was going to be a place I would remember for a long time.

If I had known then the nature of these predicted memories, I would have made the driver turn around right there and then and take me to wait for the next ferry back to the mainland.

The villa was approached through a set of ancient-looking wrought iron gates leading onto a sweeping gravel drive. The taxi stopped in front of a pair of heavy blue-painted doors set into the whitewashed stone wall of the villa. I opened the door of the car before the driver had time to do so for me and stepped out into this dream that had become a reality. There was a gentle breeze rustling the leaves of the olive trees and I took great gulps of the fresh free air as the doors opened and a young woman stood smiling at me.

'Welcome!' She came forward to take my suitcase from the driver, but I got there first, having so recently rediscovered the pleasure of carrying my own luggage. She raised her eyebrows and smiled again as I quickly paid the driver, making sure I gave him a good tip. Maria, as she cheerfully told me she was called, led me through the double doors into a stone-paved courtyard with a swimming pool surrounded by citrus trees planted in big old earthenware olive jars and an uninterrupted view of the bay below. The far edge of the water in the swimming pool melded almost imperceptibly with the clear blue sea and, even before I'd seen the rest of the villa with its stone-arched veranda hung with white muslin curtains flapping gently in the breeze, I knew I'd made the right choice.

Maria showed me around the villa and discreetly left, telling me to call her if I needed anything but that otherwise I would be left alone. She had left some fresh fruit, wine, cheese and bread in the kitchen. There was a shop in the village, she said, about a ten minutes stroll away, and most other things could be delivered if I gave her enough notice. I was intoxicated with the simplicity of it. After she had gone, I wandered from room to room, admiring the rough stone walls and whitewashed plaster offset with yards and yards of linen in pastel hues. I unpacked, stowing my clothes in the heavy wooden chest of drawers and wardrobe in the bedroom, then stripped off my travelling clothes, ran outside and dived naked into the pool. I swam a few lengths, then stopped to get my breath back, gazing across the surface of the water that appeared to meet the sea far below. The sun was already making its descent towards the horizon, becoming orange then rose red as it prepared to fuse with the illuminated runway its reflection had created.

Later, as I drifted off to sleep with the curtains billowing gently at the open French windows leading out to the courtyard, I berated myself for not having staged my escape sooner. This solitary exile had a sweeter taste than I could have dared to predict.

Even though tonight's Night Delivery is the eleventh, I can't detach myself from the fact that it is a person. He is a person. We all, I suppose, have the desire to leave something behind, make our lives mean something. But to do it in this way? How desperate does a person need to be to go to those lengths?

How desperate am I?

I was awoken in the early hours of the morning from my blissful slumber by a gunshot followed by a splash. I sat bolt upright and wondered for a moment where I was before I remembered that I was in a villa on a Greek island. I had escaped! I was free! But the gunshot had sounded very close. I slipped out from between the crisp cotton sheets, pulled a towel around my waist and rushed to the open French windows. I flicked on the switch for the courtyard floodlights a split second before realizing that there might be a crazed gunman outside with me in his – now illuminated – sights. Before I could turn them off again, I caught sight of a naked body floating face down in the pool. A body that was to become The Body in the Pool.

This was the first I knew of the incident that would make headline news.

The Shooting had occurred.

The Cell

F

I still can't say with any degree of certainty what happened immediately after I discovered The Body in the Pool. I've been over it so many times, I have no idea whether or not I noticed the remains of several lines of cocaine and a rolled up twenty euro note on the small round mosaic-topped table. I've seen the photographs of it, so I can visualize it, but I'm still not sure whether or not I saw it at the time.

So what *do* I remember? I remember vividly the extent of the full moon: it was August and the largest of the year. I recall the way the moon's reflection on the surface of the water rippled slightly, probably from the repercussions of the body falling into it or possibly from the slight breeze that made the waxen leaves of the potted citrus trees flutter, but I have almost no recollection of the actual physical appearance of The Body.

There were no reports on the news today about human bodies being pulled out of the Thames.

I was taken to the local police station, which was a small room attached to the house where the policeman lived. It appeared to have not been used much. The stone walls had been painted with coat after coat of whitewash and a pair of cotton curtains with an unsuccessfully optimistic design of blue, green and mauve turtles hung at the small window through which I could see the night sky. A single light bulb, which in retrospect should have seemed threatening but wasn't at the time, dangled into the middle of the room. The policeman – a jovial chap who introduced himself as Spiro – confessed that he had never encountered an incident like this before and wasn't sure what to do. He had telephoned to the mainland for assistance and seemed to be unable to make a decision to do anything other than wait for it to arrive. Maria, the villa's housekeeper, had been contacted and was also on her way. I was sure, at the time, that her arrival – and subsequent confirmation that I had arrived on my own – would put an end to the speculation that was clearly going on. It would all be cleared up and explained soon enough, I thought. After all, I hadn't done anything wrong. I had just had the misfortune to unwittingly play host to a suicidal intruder.

What is right and what is wrong? Adherence to a religion and its rules helps immensely with answering this question, but only if the said religion is believed in completely and unquestioningly. My mistake was to believe that, by telling the truth, the mess in which I had found myself would be cleared up. Looking back now, I get angry and hurt at my naivety. It strengthens my resolve to stick to my plan. It is what I have set out to do and it must be done. Without a plan, my existence would be empty, meaningless and without purpose. With a plan, every day can bring me one step closer to seeing it through to fruition.

In the days immediately after The Shooting, I really began to think that I had lost my mind.

Maria eventually arrived at the police station and assured me that she would find an English-speaking lawyer. I forced myself to remain calm, acknowledging that the last thing I needed was to become dramatic.

It was almost dawn by the time the lawyer arrived. Shafts of light were piercing the flimsy turtle curtains, projecting eerie angular patterns onto the rough white walls. He strode in, introduced himself as Dionysius Joannides, and set about detailing the 'crime', as he put it, in fluent but heavily-accented English. A swarthy, thickset man with large tanned hands, he fiddled with a set of amber worry beads as he spoke. It looked, he said, as if we were dealing with suicide rather than murder. I felt equal measures of shock and relief at the same time: shock that there was even a possibility that I could be accused of murder and relief that the possibility had, more than likely, already been discounted. Police officers were examining the scene of the crime at that very moment, he said, and they would shortly be removing the body. I asked if they had identified it yet. Dionysius looked at me in complete puzzlement. 'You don't know the name of this man?' He tilted his head towards me and furrowed his brow while allowing the merest hint of a smile to play on his lips.

'Of course not.' I was justifiably indignant. 'I have no idea who he was or where he came from.' The lawyer's smile began to develop. I took a deep breath. 'The first I knew of this man was when I was awoken by a gunshot and came out to find the body floating in the pool.' Dionysius cleared his throat and flicked the worry beads against his thigh.

'And the cocaine?'

Two uncommunicative policemen took me on the ferry to the mainland in handcuffs. One of them even had to come into the toilet cubicle with me. This utterly degrading incident acted as a catalyst for the familiar – but usually controlled – dark cloud of despair to begin to fold its all-pervading presence around me. Dionysius didn't believe me. Worse than that, he didn't seem inclined to even *try* to believe me. As the ferry clanked into port at the very same place in which I had – in a moment of happy abandon – toyed with the idea of throwing my luggage away, I felt my life – or at least the reasons for it – draining away. But the despondency I felt then was nothing compared with that which engulfed me when we arrived at the prison.

The cell was almost too cell-like to be real: more like something created, in its distressed authenticity, for the set of a film of the 'Midnight Express' genre. The grey-green rock walls, inset with iron rings the purpose of which I shuddered to contemplate, were streaked with dark mould and the only natural light came through a small square window dissected by two vertical bars. The floor was of dark, almost black, stone and the only furniture was an iron bed with a thin hard mattress covered in filthy striped cotton ticking.

I had been there for what seemed like days, but was actually just over eight hours, when Dionysius arrived, still dangling his amber beads. He brusquely brought out a sheaf of papers and leafed through them, shaking his head as he did so. 'It is not looking good for you,' he said, causing my heart to sink and reality to slip further from my grasp. He continued, dismally, to lecture me on what a serious offence cocaine possession was before dropping in, alarmingly casually, that it would be in my best interests to agree to a blood test, which could determine whether or not I had been using the drug. A glimmer of hope appeared before me and I readily agreed.

Dionysius then told me they had identified the dead man from a passport found in the pocket of his jeans. His name, he said – looking at me as if it was going to come as no surprise – was Richard Dingell. I shrugged or, looking back, I think I shrugged, as the name genuinely meant nothing to me.

As Dionysius left, I honestly believed that this would all soon be sorted out. I was even wondering how I would go about suing the Greek police for harassment, wrongful arrest and whatever else would be relevant. I was still travelling under the very British assumption that police procedure in all European member states was bound by some common code of practice. I was very wrong, but it was at least a conviction onto which I could cling at that time when, in the absence of any religious proclivities, I desperately needed some faith. My belief in myself was filtering away, threatening to leave me with nothing.

I admire people – if a little scornfully – who can adhere to one system of belief no matter what occurs to shake it.

Stella kept telling me, in the dirty and hope-devouring cell, that a whole sequence of possible events had really happened and that I was in denial. 'You were having a gay love affair,' she said in a matter-of-fact tone. 'I can't blame you, when you've been putting up with Roni all these years.' She went silent for a while and I thought she had finished. I was wrong. 'Why else would you come to Greece in secret?' I could see her point. Is this how it would look to the outside world? 'I've got to hand it to you, that villa was the perfect place to choose,' she continued. 'A little bit of paradise away from the prying eye. Shame you fell out and shot him!'

'Don't be ridiculous!' My retort was spoken out loud, even though her words were heard only by me.

'It's not only a river in Egypt,' she said smugly.

'What isn't?' My head was threatening to explode.

'Denial!' She cackled delightedly.

'Stella, please don't!' I pleaded. 'I need you to believe me.'

'So you need me now, do you?' Her tone was calculating. 'What about all those times you took her side against me?'

'Maybe I was wrong.'

'Maybe?' She laughed again. '*Maybe*? We didn't need her and you know it.'

'I don't know anything any more.' I put my head in my hands and closed my eyes, but it didn't stop her voice.

'You know the truth has a way of coming out sooner or later.' Her raucous voice grated inside my head. 'Was it suicide or murder?'

'I'd never seen the man before!' I shouted. I couldn't get away from her, couldn't understand what was happening, couldn't *believe* that it was happening.

'I don't mean him,' she said with a hint of exasperation in her voice, 'I mean Roni's mother.'

Do I *really* admire people who can adhere to one system of belief no matter what occurs to test their faith? The near similarities and colliding contradictions in the holy books of the world could be seen to back each other up. To me, however, they seem to collectively collude to disprove all – leaving only the bare fact that it is man's great need for something in which to believe that created religion of any sort in the first place. How can a belief that Jesus was born in a stable to a virgin impregnated by a deity survive in the light of evidence to the contrary? It must be because the need to believe is, on the whole, stronger than the desire for truth. The ability to believe in an all-seeing outside force – whether good or evil – negates the need to believe in oneself. Ironically, the need to believe and the desire for the truth have conspired in the past to make some of the most harmful and repercussive untruths in the history of the world.

Dionysius came back in what I think were the early hours of the morning; at any rate, there was no daylight permeating the small barred window, no shafts of light illuminating sections of the dirty brown walls which – no word of a lie – were scarred with small scratches in groups of four vertical, one diagonal, apparently marking off someone else's time spent in the hopeless hell hole. I tried not to imagine being there for thirty-two days as this poor soul evidently had been. But what had happened after that? Had his imprisonment been a mistake as well? In my mind's eye, I could picture myself marking off the days, weeks and even years by scratching at the wall with my fingernails, being forced to draw blood rather than lose track of time.

I heard the commotion, recognizing my lawyer's voice as he argued with the guards who were clearly putting up some resistance to letting him see me. Thankfully he seemed to be taking no notice of them whatsoever and I got to my feet in anticipation, convinced he was coming to tell me that he had realized – and persuaded the police – that my incarceration was all a terrible mistake and that I was free to go. I would be released and it would all be sorted out without Roni ever finding out. That was my belief and I was clinging to it. It had kept me going up to that point.

Does it really and truly matter whether or not The Resurrection actually happened? Does it make it any less useful as a tool of belief? Fiction, as long as it is recognized as such, can be every bit as uplifting as fact, but does the level of fiction in The Bible need to be acknowledged in order to appreciate its genuine beauty?

Dionysius looked at me and sighed heavily as he was shown into the cell. The door clattered shut behind him; he made as if to sit down then, looking at the filthy surface he would be sitting on, seemed to think better of it and straightened himself again to a full standing position. He cleared his throat and looked at me. 'The dead man,' he said, 'has a tattoo.' Having taken in the gravity of his expression, I had been expecting something terrible – at the very least that a court had sentenced me to thirty years imprisonment without a trial – so I think I must have smiled. But my smiled disappeared as Dionysius continued with a grave expression on his face. 'The tattoo on the dead man's left buttock was of a name.' He paused. '*Your* name, in fact.' I was momentarily stunned, then realized after a moment's thought that it was nothing more than a coincidence.

'Surely that doesn't prove anything?' My desperate indignation clearly hit the wrong note.

'You don't think so?' It was at this point that Dionysius seemed to give up on me. This corpse, bearing my name and thus evidence of my guilt as if I had signed it myself, was clearly – in his eyes – that of my dead lover whom I had plied with cocaine before either shooting him or watching him shoot himself. Indignation began to give way to despair. It was a dark despair that threatened to permeate every part of my being, the like of which I hadn't experienced for many years.

And that was before I had any hint of what was just around the corner.

'Be honest with me!' Dionysius looked me straight in the eye as he said it, slapping the amber worry beads rhythmically against his right thigh. 'Don't think I don't understand!' He spat the words out without any attempt at sounding sympathetic. 'I realize you have had to keep your sexuality secret up to this point and chose this destination in order to be out of the public eye.' Strangely enough, he didn't allude to the fact that I was – in his eyes – a married gay man, but I suppose, being Greek, he would be no stranger to that phenomenon. 'Your mistake,' he told me sternly, 'was to think you could get away with bringing drugs to our country. It will not be tolerated!' The amber beads clattered noisily as they fell on the dirty stone floor and I realized – for the first time – the full extent of the trouble I was in.

Does the end always justify the means? Or, to put it another way, does the end *ever* justify the means? Is it possible to forgive and forget? Remembering the way I felt in the prison cell that night after Dionysius picked up his beads and left, I would say – very emphatically – no.

'You're losing your mind!' It was Stella again. Her ranting woke me in the middle of the night shortly after I'd finally managed to fall asleep. 'It's no wonder you don't know who you are! You allowed that bitch to make you into a caricature of yourself.' I couldn't have argued with her, even if I'd had the energy. 'You're little more than a construct of someone else's imagination!'

What was she then?

Just before Dionysius arrived with his latest bombshell the next day, Stella was sneeringly arguing with my conviction that I was an unfortunate victim of circumstance – that a peculiar and clearly disturbed person had wandered into the grounds of my villa late at night, taken drugs and shot himself. 'And he just *happened* to have your name tattooed on his backside?' According to her, there was no logic or reason attached to my version of events and I was deluding myself. 'You're living in a dream world!' And this from a character who says she married a butcher because she was 'impressed by the size of his chopper' and thinks that the audience liked her rasping off-key singing, rather than that they were amazed she had the nerve to do it at all. 'Reality will dawn soon, my boy,' she said scathingly, before disappearing right on cue as the sound of beads clanking against a muscular thigh came closer. If I had known then what Dionysius was about to tell me, I might have tried to follow Stella to wherever it is she goes, leaving just a vacant body – an empty husk – in that cell.

Dionysius entered with a grave expression on his face and slapped down a copy of a British daily tabloid (the most conservative and my least favourite) open at a page emblazoned with a photograph – blurred but discernible – depicting me on the ferry handcuffed to one of the two policemen flanking me.

'Danny's Double Life Denied' read the headline, accompanied by a piece describing Roni's denial of my having a secret gay existence, a drug habit and a suicidal gay lover. A tourist had apparently spotted and photographed me on the ferry, then sold the photograph to the highest bidder, who had subsequently contacted Roni for her comment on the situation. My hopes that this predicament in which I had found myself could be sorted out without Roni finding out had obviously been hopelessly futile.

The piece described the alleged happenings in vivid and unstinting detail, making me mystified as to the source of the information, but it was the staunch denial from Roni that rang the first tinkling hint of the first of many warning bells that were to sound in my head.

Dionysius looked down at me in a condescending fashion. 'You are lucky you have the support of your wife.' His voice conveyed his deep disdain for my perceived behaviour. I had realized by now that he wasn't the ally I had hoped – and could be forgiven for having expected – he would be. 'Tonight we will have the results of your drug test.' He shook his head again, clearly already having condemned me in his mind.

No matter how hard I try, I can't remember what I truly thought and believed at that time. Did I honestly think that the dead man having my name tattooed on his body was a coincidence? Did I really believe that an opportunistic tourist had recognized and photographed me on that ferry? I do know that Roni's reported reaction made me uneasy, but did I have any true grasp of the lengths she had gone to?

'If you throw away what we've got together, you'll live to regret it!'

I like to think now that her words were already ringing in my ears at that time, but that presupposes that I was thinking clearly. I was incarcerated in a Greek jail on suspicion of a crime I most certainly hadn't committed. My chief concern was, understandably, how I was going to get out of my immediate dilemma. The human mind has a defence mechanism it uses at times like these which enable it to concentrate on one thing at a time.

Dionysius returned later that evening, the look of severe disapproval still on his face. 'You are a very lucky man,' he said.

'Am I?' It was hardly surprising that I failed to share his sentiment.

'The drug test was negative.' He paused, while I wondered whether I was alone in knowing that this owed nothing to luck. With a slight shake of his head, he managed to betray his belief that I had got away with something. 'All your luggage was also screened and swabbed. They found no traces of cocaine.'

'So?' I suppose I was waiting for an apology, if not for him to give credence to my belief that the dead man was a deranged stalker. No apology or explanation was forthcoming.

'You will be released.' The beads clanked against his thigh. 'Without charge.' The relief I knew I should have been feeling was tainted by the fear of what lay ahead. 'It has been requested that the body of your... that the body is returned to England.' I wanted to express my anger at his continued assumptions and insinuations, but took a deep breath and stood up quietly.

'Wait!' Dionysius put his hand on my arm and guided me back to a sitting position. 'The condition of your release is that you leave Greece immediately.' I almost laughed. Did he really imagine that I wanted to stay in the country in which I had experienced this torment for one moment longer than necessary? 'Immediately.' I had heard him the first time. 'Your luggage has been brought here and your wife has organized a flight back to Italy. Tonight.'

The outfit I have chosen in which to greet tonight's Night Delivery was made for Roni to wear at the end of our second wedding. It was a going away outfit (purely for photographic purposes, since we didn't have time to go on a honeymoon). Low-waisted, it is cut from beige and dark brown linen and has a matching head-hugging hat that was designed to make her look young, fresh and hopeful like a bride of some eighty years earlier.

How often appearances can deceive, especially when they are specifically designed to do exactly that.

The letter 'F' – copied from the sixth volume of an incomplete Macklin Bible I bought from a collector in Lewes with some of the plentiful proceeds of the second television series – is laid out with the needle and ink, soon to become another character in the epitaph, another piece fitted into the jigsaw as my plan nears completion.
I can count the days now on the fingers of one hand. It is a countdown to the end.

The Palazzo

A policeman for whose uncommunicative nature I was very grateful accompanied me on my journey back to the airport. He had evidently been entrusted with the task of making sure I got on the plane to Florence and seemed relieved that I didn't put up any resistance. I was too tired to do anything else, using what little energy I had left to concentrate on getting to my suite at the palazzo where I would be able to have a long bath and wash away the stench of the prison cell. I still ask myself what was going through my mind on that journey, but I know that the answer is simple. Conspiracy theories hadn't had a look in yet. My concentration was purely and simply focussed on the anticipation of that bath.

It helped me endure the horror of sitting on an aeroplane in close proximity to other passengers knowing that I smelt like an incontinent tramp. It helped me to believe that the driver who met me at the airport in Florence knew nothing of my Greek humiliation, even though this was extremely unlikely.

We left the motorway and drove through villages almost too beautiful to be genuine, too perfect in their haphazard juxtaposition of mellow stonework, creeping vineyards and blooming flowers. Was all this real or was I imagining it to get away from the horror of my existence?

A sign for the hotel, which I hoped was not an apparition, signalled that we were nearly there. I saw it on the horizon – a hilltop fortification that seemed to be trying to whisper to me of the centuries through which its rambling ramparts had been built. In its shadow, I felt the brevity and insignificance of my time on earth. We approached the palazzo along a long steep road banked on either side with ancient stone walls, leading to an arch in a clock tower. I looked up at the long windows set into the thick castellated walls and, as I was driven through the arch, was unable to deny the existence of a strong feeling that I had left the confines of one prison for those of another.

I held on to the anticipation of that bath, using it to help me endure the polite deferential behaviour of the uniformed porter who came to collect my luggage and the humiliatingly knowing look I got from the alarmingly well-groomed man at the reception desk as he spoke to me. 'Everything has been done to assure *total* privacy during your stay, sir.' His words made me wince. I nodded dumbly and followed the porter through lofty corridors adorned with oil paintings ostentatious in their faded antiquity and out into a paved courtyard, at the centre of which was a large stone well whose depths I couldn't help but imagine falling away beneath the solid ground I was walking on.

He led the way into the old stable block, the bright sunshine giving way to cool shadows playing on exposed chestnut beams, delicately colour-washed to fit with their new setting as luxurious hotel accommodation rather than livestock sheds. We arrived at my suite. More exposed beams, clay roof tiles and rough lime render formed a backdrop for opulent embroidered curtains, tapestries, carpets and delicate Venetian chandeliers sending their speckled reflections dancing around the cool, airy expensive rooms, which reminded me of our Mews house – blatantly masquerading as something they weren't (or at least weren't designed to be).

Looking back, I suppose I should have felt some affinity, should have drawn some comfort from these old buildings being forced into an alien use, but all that kept me going was the thought of that cleansing bath. It helped me hide my reaction to seeing the British tabloid newspapers arranged in subtle blatancy on the carved chest serving as a coffee table.

It would be more truthful to say that I managed to hide my reaction until the porter closed the door behind himself leaving me alone. Using all my remaining energy to put one foot in front of the other, I walked into the vast bathroom, sank to the cold flag-stoned floor beside the enormous roll-top bath, put my head in my hands and wept like a baby.

I don't know how long I spent on that floor. Time passing was the least of my worries. But I came back to my senses to hear the telephone ringing. I got up from the floor and answered it without thinking who might be calling. 'Hello.'

'Danny.' I recognized the voice immediately. It belonged to Rodney Markham, the lawyer who was on the payroll of Danron Productions.

'Hello Rodney,' I said with instinctive politeness, not having had the chance to think about how I would be expected to greet him.

'Have you seen the newspapers?' Rather than question how he knew I had the newspapers, I felt a stab of childish guilt that I hadn't read them yet.

'I was about to have a bath.' My reply must have sounded petulant.

'Things are not looking good.' He sounded somehow apologetic and embarrassed. 'I'm at Heathrow airport. I will be with you by late this evening.'

'Oh.'

'Please wait up for me. We need to talk.' I could sense that he was as eager to talk to me as I was to listen to him.

'Ok.'

'Read the papers.' He cleared his throat. 'You need to.'

'Thanks Rodney.' What was I thanking him for? For wordlessly making me feel responsible for my predicament?

'They're currently performing an autopsy on the body. It arrived back in this country earlier today.' I had no idea of the response he was expecting, so refrained from giving one. 'Danny?'

'Yes?'

'See you later.' The line went dead and I walked slowly over to the neatly arranged newspapers.

All three of the tabloids carried a front page story describing the alleged happenings in Greece. The first one I picked up carried an exclusive interview with the dead man's mother, Mrs Brenda Dingell: *"'Ricky was a bit of a drifter and had had problems in the past – but he was very excited about the fact that this new relationship he was having was the real thing. We had accepted him for what he was a long time ago and he assured me that he was going to make his life mean something. Of course, we were sworn to secrecy, what with him being involved with a celebrity and all that." Mrs Dingell paused to dab her eyes with a handkerchief. "I'm ashamed to say we didn't really believe him until he came home with the new car."'*

I was later to discover that the mentioned car was paid for from my bank account almost a month earlier. But that first day in the palazzo suite I was still in relative ignorance of the facts. But that ignorance was anything but blissful.

Mrs Dingell went on to describe her son's long battle with manic depression – something she felt must have been brought to the fore by mixing with *"a self-centred megalomaniac celebrity who had no idea how sensitive he was."* She had, she said, been looking forward to meeting her son's new boyfriend, but now hoped that he *"burned in hell where he belonged."* The interviewer had then tagged on her comment that *"celebrities seem to think they have the right to make a mockery of everything us ordinary folk hold dear... and he had a wife too."*

Once again, I'm unable to genuinely recount what I was feeling as I read those words. I could say that I was confused, disbelieving and bewildered. But that could equally be what I would now expect myself to have been feeling. I think it would be more honest to say that I felt completely numb.

The next bit of the article sent an involuntary chill through my body. While still worded carefully to keep within legal boundaries, it stated as boldly as it could that the family expected whoever was responsible for Ricky's death to *"stand trial like any normal person would have to on his return to the UK."*

A small story further on in the same newspaper featured a Soho tattooist who claimed to have been responsible for the 'Danny' tattoo sported by the dead man. *'"He chatted away while I was doing it," said Vernon Quigley (53), whose tattoo parlour in bustling Brewer Street in London's Soho lists several celebrities amongst its clients. "It certainly didn't strike me that he was the kind of chap who was about to top himself. He told me it was his boyfriend's name and that he wanted to show everyone how much he meant to him. I didn't like to ask how many people were likely to see his backside," added Mr Quigley with a hastily suppressed grin.'*

The next paper had a front page story – coupled with a large and very flattering photograph of Roni in a beautifully tailored suit and dark glasses – outlining her *'shock, disappointment and complete lack of belief'* at the allegations that her husband had been leading a secret gay double life. It detailed, in words that I must admit I could hear her saying, that ours had been a *'full marriage'* and that this shattering event could not have come at a worse time. *'This whole situation is completely preposterous. There is no way my husband would jeopardize our future in this way.'*

The rest of the story – not in Roni's words – dealt with the status of Danron Productions and its planned future projects.

The third front page featured a large photograph – a much-used publicity shot with me in a checked suit looking straight at the camera in a cheeky and knowing pose – with the headline *'Danny's Drug Dependency Downfall?'* The question mark seemed to say it all. I put the newspaper tidily back on the coffee table on top of the others, then turned it over. I didn't want to look myself in the eye.

I needed that bath.

Apparently, people who are genuinely insane think that they are perfectly well adjusted and that the rest of the world is behaving irrationally. It crossed my mind – albeit fleetingly – that this was the case with me. To make matters worse, Stella's voice suddenly cut into my thoughts. 'It's your fault for siding with that bitch against me in the first place!' Her spiteful words made me wonder if Stella had done it, even though I knew it wasn't physically possible.

Steaming water gushed into the massive bathtub as I tore off my stinking clothes. I didn't need to read the story accompanying that last headline to know what it said. I cast my mind back to what had seemed, at the time, a ludicrous tactic.

'The public loves a flawed hero,' Roni had said. 'Isn't that right, Rex?'

'Trust me, Danny.' Rex had even put his hand on my shoulder like some dependable father-figure (even though he was less than ten years older than me).

And it had worked. I had been forgiven for having a drug and alcohol dependency, even though it was a manufactured one. The public had admired my ability to overcome these obstacles and taken me to their hearts. I had been propelled to fame and fortune beyond my wildest dreams, not to mention well beyond my desires.

But the public was, as always, like an unreliable dog that can at any time swing around and bite you on the backside. Weren't these the same people for whom I used to wait behind the curtains, having prepared myself with the material I needed, the bare facts necessary, the raw ingredients of what was to become – in my alchemist's hands – the performance that would amuse them, make them laugh and bring them alive for that time I was there in front of them? What had I done to make them so eager to bay for my blood?

I climbed into the bath, hoping my immersion in its soapy warmth would make some sense of the disparate and seemingly illogical facts with which I was faced. The cleansing liquid merely served to make me feel more hemmed in, more than ever a prisoner of circumstance (as well as a detainee in this over-decorated castle). I sank down into the water, letting its surface close over my face, the momentary deprivation of oxygen still not acting as a catalyst to understanding. How the hell had all this happened? I had escaped to Greece without anyone knowing where I was going. Then a dead body – with my name indelibly etched on it – had appeared floating face down in the pool of my remote villa. And now this story had emerged that the man, who was to become The Body in the Pool, had told his family that he was dating a celebrity. It couldn't all be coincidence, could it? What was I missing?

The confused events, thoughts and emotions continued to churn in my exhausted brain, my thoughts swirling inexorably down towards the dark forbidding depths it was unwise to let myself revisit. As the water grew gradually colder, the darkness beckoned to me to give in to it, to admit defeat. But to what, or whom, would I be surrendering?

'What have you got to lose?' Roni used to say.
What had I got to lose?

I leaped up out of the now tepid water as realization dawned and the curtain began to lift. The first brick was knocked out of the wall that stood between me and the truth. A glimmer of hope shone through. I was suddenly in no doubt whatsoever that this was a war being waged on me. If I wasn't going to take it lying down, I had to confirm my suspicions about the identity of my adversary and fight back.

I hastily threw on a soft towelling robe over my damp body and felt a heat building inside as I rushed to the computer, which was artfully concealed in a large armoire with the television, video and DVD player. Efficiently delivered onto the information super highway, I typed the URL for Danron Productions' website.

'Go on! Look at the format for the new show!' Stella goaded me as I clicked the relevant link from the home page. I saw that the title of 'Danny's Talent Quest' had been altered to 'Launch Pad'. I scrolled through the proposed format of the show, which was apparently due to go into production later in the year. My fears were confirmed when I saw that Roni – well on the way to being a personality in her own right thanks to the publicity surrounding my downfall – was to be the vehicle and star. 'See!' Stella was triumphant. 'I *told* you she was going to make a career out of this, didn't I?'

'Danny.' Rodney, a once-handsome man now greying at the temples and emanating an air of efficient frustration, strode into the suite wearing a travel-crumpled dark suit and thrust the hand that wasn't holding his black brief case towards me to shake mine. His tired, dark-circled eyes looked around the room. I got the impression he was trying to look anywhere but at my face.

'Rodney.' I motioned for him to sit down and followed suit.

'Let me run through the state of play at the moment, then I'll answer your questions.' He opened his briefcase, took out a sheaf of papers and glanced at his watch.

'Got a flight to catch?' I didn't mean it to come out so flippantly. Rodney gave me a dark look. Or at least he tried to, but his eyes seemed to focus on the swathe of tapestry to the right of my head.

'The results of the post mortem came through while I was en route.' He moved his head as if to look at me, still making sure our eyes didn't meet, then obviously thought better of it, looked down at his papers and continued. 'The dead man had recently been sodomized.' He didn't add 'by you', but he didn't need to. 'There were traces of semen found inside the body.'

('Now you're fucked,' Stella said in my head. Then I heard her raucous cackling laugh as she corrected herself. 'Oops, my mistake – it appears that he was!')

Rodney seemed perturbed by my silence. If he thought that the statement was going to elicit a response – or maybe a confession – from me, he was very much mistaken. 'Do you realize what that means?' He looked at the curtains near my head again.

'Yes, Rodney, I'm hardly likely to have reached the age of thirty five without having become acquainted with the definition of sodomy.'

'I'm rather afraid I can't share your flippancy.' He gave me what Iris would have called an 'old-fashioned look' before clearing his throat and continuing. 'His family are making a big fuss and attempting to involve the British police.' He didn't even look up to see if I was registering fear. It would have involved looking into my eyes.

I stood up and walked over to the window to look out into the darkness. I couldn't see what I knew was there – a rolling vista of olive groves and vineyards sweeping down towards the town in the valley below. My movement clearly made him uneasy. Without hurrying I went back to my seat and became still again to allow him to continue with his script. 'It would be very much in your interests to volunteer a DNA sample to eliminate you from suspicion.'

'Suspicion of what?' I asked. Rodney cleared his throat and came out with an involuntary splutter. 'Would you like a glass of water?' I stood up and moved as if to get one, noting his discomfort at I came closer to him.

'No... thank you.' He kept his eyes on the papers in front of him. I noticed that his hands were shaking. 'Do I need to spell it out?'

'You think I fucked him, shot him and pushed him in the pool?'

'What *I* think is not the issue in question at the moment.' His knee jerked and some of the papers fell on the Aubusson carpet under his feet.

'Am I meant to be relieved by that?'

'Danny, your co-operation would be beneficial to your predicament at the moment.'

'So you want a DNA sample? Give me a bottle and I'll perform.'

'Please!' He blushed crimson. 'A simple mouth swab will suffice.'

'Sorry.' I didn't mean it. 'But surely they won't accept your word for it that the sample came from me?'

'I've brought a police officer with me who is authorized to establish your identity and take the sample.'

'Roni's certainly pulling some strings for me isn't she?' It was the first time her name had been mentioned since his arrival. His left arm jerked with the spasmodic action of a badly-operated marionette. I decided to make things easier for him and reverted to my expected role. 'Of course I'll give a DNA sample. I'll do anything that will help to get me out of this unfortunate mess.'

'You will?' His shoulders sank down in a visible sign of relief.

'Of course. What have I got to lose?' I gave him an appealing look, but he didn't show any signs of having seen it. 'Go and get your policeman.'

'There's one more thing.' I could see him taking a deep breath.

'Yes?' I had a strong sense that I knew what was coming.

'If your DNA matches the—'

'It won't!' I was as emphatic as Roni had no doubt told him I was likely to be.

'My advice to you would be to safeguard against any potential legal action by the family of the... er...

deceased.' His delivery of the script was becoming less fluent.

'*If* the DNA matches?' I stood up again and watched him flinch. 'Since it isn't going to, do we really need to discuss this?'

'I'm merely trying to safeguard your own property and that of Danron Productions in the event that—'

'You mean I need to make sure I don't own anything?' I shook my head in mock confusion, despite having predicted his imminent proposal. 'You're surely not suggesting that I give away all my property and assets?'

'What I have here,' he fumbled in the briefcase again, 'is a document which, if you signed it, would only be used in the event—'

'That my DNA matches that of the semen found in the dead body,' I interrupted. 'So, bearing in mind the fact that I know that my DNA cannot possibly match that of the semen found in,' I paused momentarily and watched Rodney physically squirm, 'the dead man, there is very little point in me signing it.'

While it may be memory working its mischief again, I like to think that at this point I was actually beginning to take pride – if not pleasure – in my performance.

Rodney replaced all his papers in the briefcase and stood up, the evidence of his weariness clearly visible.

'I can't force you to sign it.'

'But your role is to advise me?'

'Of course.' The hint of resentment in his tone was badly disguised. 'The first duty of the lawyer is to...'

'Well since you put it like that,' I stated, knowing that he hadn't yet. 'I suppose there's no harm in safeguarding our assets against every eventuality.'

'But you said—'

'For goodness' sake Rodney! Can't you make allowances for the fact I've been nearly driven out of my mind by the events of the last few days?'

'Of course I can!' He looked uneasy.

'Sit back down and show me what I'm meant to sign.' It was the cue he needed. He followed my suggestion and began to run through the document.

Five minutes later I signed on the dotted line, gifting all of my assets – which consisted of my half of the apartment, the cash in my bank accounts and my shares in Danron Productions – to Roni in the event that the DNA test proved positive. 'Just a safeguard against the dead man's family pursuing legal action against you,' he said as he snapped the briefcase shut.

'Of course,' I agreed. 'Now go and get your policeman and let's get this over with.' He nodded and scuttled out through the door. I looked at the dent he had left in the sofa cushions and ruminated on the fact that, throughout the proceedings, he hadn't made even a remote attempt to solicit my version of the events in Greece. Nor had he explained how he had managed to get the document drafted, prepared and printed when – by his own admission – he had only heard about the results of the autopsy when en route to Italy.

I wasn't surprised when I sensed Stella's imminent return. I had been expecting her. 'You're going to let them take a DNA sample?' She spat the words out. 'Are you completely deranged?' It was with great relief that I realized I didn't feel the need to answer her. Stella was not my adversary. But I was in no doubt who was. And, if I was to have a hope in hell of beating her, I was going to have to let her think she was winning.

Stella had fortunately gone again by the time Rodney came back with his policeman and the swab was taken. They departed – two more characters in this drama with a plot worthy of the great Agatha Christie – leaving me to get on with the process of lateral thinking. My intention was to let Rodney go back and report to Roni that I was taking it lying down. Just as I was almost certain that my DNA would match up with the sperm found in the body, I knew that there was a riddle to solve and that I could solve it. *How* I was going to solve it was another matter.

The first step, I realized, was to get back to London without being expected. The element of surprise was of paramount importance. There was no doubt in my mind whatsoever that Roni would be informed the moment I left the palazzo. I was a prisoner.

Just then, a knock came at my door. 'Room service, sir.' I opened the door and ushered in the eager young waiter bearing my dinner on a trolley. Delicious smells wafted towards me as he unloaded the meal – which consisted of a mouth-watering array of antipasti, fresh pasta and salad – onto a small table by the window and uncorked a bottle of red wine. I had hardly eaten since my arrival at the Greek villa and knew that my thought processes were suffering as a result. Some nourishment would go a long way to helping me find a way out. 'In one hour, I will come back to take away the plates.'

'Your English is very good.' My taste buds were anticipating the treat in store for them.

'Thank you sir.' He was a handsome young man, probably no more than nineteen years old. His whole life was ahead of him. I tried to remember how I had felt at that age, my memory searching through the reams of material at its disposal. 'I am hoping to work next in London.'

'It's quite different from here.' I gazed out again at the darkness outside the window, once again imagining the landscape that I knew was there but couldn't see.

'I'm from Milan, sir, so I am used to city life.' He smiled enthusiastically. 'After London, I would like to work in Paris. Then maybe Barcelona.' So many hopes and dreams. I envied and pitied him at the same time.

'I don't suppose,' I said carefully as an idea began to form, 'that you have any time off in the next few days? I will pay you to do something for me.'

'Sir?' His eyes opened wide and he looked me up and down as I realized too late what he thought I was suggesting. 'I am off tomorrow all day after I serve breakfast, but—'

'No, no... please accept my apologies. I didn't explain myself.' I realized it was a long shot, but had started so I had to finish. I took a deep breath and told him what I wanted him to do for me.

A little over an hour later I went to bed knowing I would have a good night's sleep for the first time since The Shooting. Only twenty four hours earlier I had been in a Greek prison cell. Now I had just eaten an exquisite Italian dinner and was about to slip between the crisp cotton sheets of a seventeenth century four poster bed screened from the room by beautifully embroidered tapestry curtains.

And I had the beginnings of a plan.

It all seems so long ago – the birth of the plan whose development and implementation has kept me sane for nearly three years. Now I am just two days away from seeing that plan come to its conclusion.

For tonight's Night Delivery I will be wearing one of Roni's 'wronged wife' outfits that she acquired during the time I was in Greece and Italy. A tailored suit in a deep aubergine, it will be worn with a simple blouse in white wild silk. The shoes are a work of art in themselves – intricately-strapped Jimmy Choos in the same colour as the suit. For all her faults, Roni certainly knows about clothes.

Becoming Roni is different from becoming Stella. With Roni, I choose what my version of her is going to wear, what she is going to do and say, but succeed in making each action and word convincing because I know exactly how her mind works, know exactly what she would do and say in any given situation. With Stella, I don't have to 'make' her convincing. She erupts into volatile life like a volcano that has been lurking below the surface, bubbling and seething.

As with all of the Night Deliveries, I have planned every detail meticulously. The call comes to Roni's mobile ten minutes before each one is due to arrive and it is only at that point that I give out the address. The money is always dealt with on arrival. I make sure the transfer by internet banking (from Roni's account of course) is completely straightforward and visible to the recipient. After all, they need to know that their last will and testament will have the anticipated substance if they are to die in anything approaching peace. It has surprised me that there have been no mistakes, no changes of mind, no desperate last minute pleadings. But, on the other hand, I am no doubt downplaying my ability to plan and prepare. There is – and I can't stress this enough – no substitute for adequate preparation.

Whatever interpretation could be put on these nocturnal activities, they do not involve murder. And don't think that I haven't explored the possibility that they do. I'm sure there are those among you who are raising a moralistic eyebrow or wagging a didactic finger. In anticipation of this, I can honestly tell you that these people have been carefully chosen. What binds them together is an individually arrived at decision that their lives are no longer worth living. I have given them a chance to bequeath something to those they leave behind. I wouldn't go as far as saying that it gives their lives some meaning, but they earn a large sum of money from doing something they were going to do for nothing. I have never forced anyone to do anything they don't want to do. Except Roni.

The Revelation

R

The next morning, shortly after having eaten a hearty and leisurely breakfast of sliced mango, kiwi fruit and papaya with natural yoghurt followed by freshly baked bread washed down with deliciously dark and fragrant coffee, I was seen on a bicycle by local people working in the undulating vineyards flanking the winding gravel road leading away from the palazzo. Except that those who saw me didn't see me. They saw – or thought they saw – the waiter, dressed in Levi's jeans, a red and white Abercrombie and Fitch T-shirt and bright red Gant cap, riding furiously away at speed as he always did. He, or I, even waved hastily but enthusiastically to the girls in the laundry as he sped past.

Half an hour later, I was at the train station padlocking the bicycle to a rack as agreed with my conspirator who was hopefully more than happy being paid to relax in my room at the palazzo for the entire day eating the regular meals I had taken the trouble to order before I left (asking for them to be left outside the room as I didn't want to be disturbed). I had paid him handsomely for his clothes and his time. Provided he was true to his word, my departure would not be noted until the next morning.

I boarded the first train to Florence, making sure I left myself plenty of time to get to the airport. Luckily I had a superfluity of euros with which I had equipped myself to go to Greece. It was something of a novelty to be travelling so light – something I hadn't done since my student days. How much water had flowed under the proverbial bridge since then? I watched the Tuscan scenery – imagining that I was static and the breathtaking landscape was speeding past me.

While I didn't argue with my parents' assumption that my school career would be followed by three years at university – largely because I was at a loss for what else I might do with my time – I drew the line at going to Oxford, despite having been offered a place. It wasn't, I am fairly certain, that I didn't realize the honour and prestige attached to the opportunity. In fact, I think that is precisely what steered me away from this ancient seat of learning. I didn't want to be moulded into something I didn't want to be, despite not yet knowing what I *did* want to be. Perhaps I knew then the extent to which I was capable of being coerced into a way of life that would make me unhappy and frustrated due to my need to be constantly occupied.

My parents, I hasten to add, were bewildered, confused and openly angry that I could turn down what they saw as the ultimate university in favour of a lesser-known University of London college. The reasons I gave, which fell largely on deaf ears, were that I needed to develop my talents in my own way and decide on a career path of my own choosing.

'As long as you don't expect us to support you in this ludicrously woolly-headed plan,' my father shouted one night. My mother looked up from her wheelchair and shook her head sadly. I didn't reply, but used this as further motivation to prove that I could make my own way in the world.

Before my first term had started, I had secured a job behind the bar in a cabaret club. Before the end of that term, I was assisting with sound and lighting at two other clubs. By the end of my second year I was – as a result of a chance comment – hosting a comedy night once a week at yet another establishment. By the time I graduated, I was working the circuit with my own act and was renting the small flat in Battersea.

I can see now that without this peculiar occupation with which I had landed myself, those days following my graduation would have been as bleak as those spent in the Greek prison cell.

I was lucky to get a flight to Paris which was scheduled to leave in less than two hours. There was barely time to have second thoughts about the journey on which I was embarking. Would I have changed my mind if I had? Is there ever anything to be gained by asking what might have been?

What I do know is that I felt that my life had a purpose again, in the same way it had following my father's sweeping statement (which he subsequently denied having meant, while at the same time expressing anger and hurt that my allowance cheques were never paid into my account). Even at that age, I knew what I needed to keep myself from desperation and despair. Better than any medication for manic depression (or bipolarity as is now the fashion to call it) was the ability to be able to work ceaselessly towards an aim. But in order to do that, I needed to have an aim in which I wholeheartedly believed. Like the similar need for religion in others, I needed a purpose, something larger than myself towards which I could put myself under pressure to work.

Similarly, I am now working ceaselessly towards the culmination of my plan, along with the not unwelcome pressure it entails. I am glad to say that I truly believe that I am nearly there. I can't allow myself the luxury of a negative thought.

It is often said that time alone is a great healer. I tend to disagree. Time can only heal if it is used in a determined fashion to work towards a goal.

I stepped off the Eurostar at Waterloo Station, still anonymous in my newly-acquired clothes, and rode up the escalator keeping my head tilted downwards so that the peak of the cap shaded my face. It was a struggle to avert my eyes from the news stand I passed, although a morbid fascination to see whether I was still front page news threatened to drag my line of sight towards it. I breathed in the early evening London atmosphere as I stepped outside to the taxi rank.

Thankfully the queue was short and I managed to avoid eye contact with anyone – although, since they weren't expecting to see me, there was little chance of them doing so – and hailed a taxi, giving him the name of a street ten minutes walk from the apartment in my best mumbled impression of Pierce Brosnan. The cab driver began to pull away from the kerb before I had even closed the door. I was on my way.

I watched the London landmarks that should have been familiar as they passed the cab at speed. While I recognized them all – the conspicuously concrete Hayward Gallery, in whose shadow cowered the Television Centre at which I had spent so much of my recent life, the Oxo Tower and the Tate Modern (two monolithic formerly redundant structures both given new life and purpose) – the route home felt new and unknown. Was it unfamiliar just because the apartment didn't yet feel like home or because I was a very different person from the optimistic individual who had left London only a few days earlier?

The landmarks are obviously still there now, despite the fact that I haven't seen them since. While there are clearly entities that exist only in my consciousness, I firmly believe that I am not a mentalist.

'Whereabouts in Pacific Street do you want, mate?' The cab driver looked over his shoulder at me, a sudden quizzical look coming over his face as if he was about to launch into a recognition speech.

'Just on the right past the off-licence, thanks.' My incarnation of Pierce Brosnan seemed to have been spending a lot of time in Glasgow, but my efforts were rewarded as the look on the cabbie's face was replaced with a one of disappointment (that I wasn't a celebrity) followed by relief (that he hadn't got to remember who I was). I became, in his eyes, just a regular customer who bore a passing resemblance to someone he ought to have been able to recognize. Nevertheless, I was glad that I hadn't asked him to take me directly to the apartment. 'Better to be safe than sorry.' as Iris would have said. I looked at the meter and handed him the only sterling cash I had left in my wallet and made a flippant hand gesture to indicate that he could keep the change. He gave me a hasty nod and wave as he turned the cab around and merged back in with the traffic.

So far so good. I had arrived back in London without being seen or, hopefully, my entry into the country being recorded.

I set off towards the apartment with more than a slight feeling of trepidation. It had occurred to me that it was entirely possible that the press would be camped outside. 'Cross that bridge when you come to it.' Iris was now with me in spirit as I pursued my mission. Once I have set my mind on completing a task, I have the ability to see it through with a single-mindedness others can find impressive. Even though I didn't know the exact nature – beyond this first step – of the plan I was implementing, I knew that I would be able to see it through to completion, no matter how much time and determination was required.

It may be difficult to understand (and may seem like a contradiction in terms), but the self-doubting side of my nature drives me on to achieve. I have the need to prove that I have what it takes to shape my own destiny and – in order to do that – have to set myself tasks which might appear to be unrealistically ambitious to the average contented citizen. The results, though, speak for themselves. As I approached the apartment that night, I felt more alive than I had in years.

I don't bother to question any more why I drive myself so hard. It is a part of my nature that I can ignore at my peril. Presented with a challenge, I feel the need to rise to it. I can't remember a time when I didn't. It's only recently that I have had time to ruminate on the past and analyse these aspects of my character. I feel empowered by knowing what motivates me.

When I find myself searching through the carefully ordered volumes of my memories, the night I first went on stage to perform an act leaps out at me. I suppose it could be called a milestone in my career, but without my reaction to the opportunity which arose, it would have remained merely that: an opportunity. It began quite inauspiciously with my arrival at a pub in the East End expecting to host a night as I had every Wednesday for the preceding six months. I was feeling the usual trepidation at facing an audience, despite the fact that I was – as always – well prepared with plenty of material at my disposal and was familiar with the two acts billed to appear that night. The usual pre-show chat in the dressing room with the performers in question gave me no premonition of what was to happen later.

The first act was an up-and-coming comic whose dead-pan method of delivery belied his razor sharp observations of human behaviour. I had introduced him a few times before and enjoyed watching the audience gradually coming around to his individual brand of comedy. I saw it as my duty as compere to give a few hints of the act to come without spoiling any surprises or stealing from that performer's repertoire, in order to prepare the audience for what was to come. It had stood me in good stead and that evening was no different as the audience lapped up his virtually seamless monologue and showed their appreciation.

The pub was very full and my employer, the promoter, gave me a thumbs-up sign as I announced the interval, along with an allusion to what was to come in the second half. The act that I thought was to come in the second half was an extremely overweight comedienne who mixed her interpretations (I hesitate to call them impersonations) of famous singers with a bit of witty (and usually quite derogatory) observation about current affairs. I knew and liked her act. I also knew that a large proportion of the audience was there purely to see her, so realized why the promoter looked more than a little flustered when he rushed up to me ten minutes later as I was sipping at what I saw as a well-earned pint of lager to tell me that she had just been hit by a double decker bus on her way back from the fish and chip shop over the road. 'What the fuck am

I going to do?' He ran a hand through his hair as he looked at the rowdy and inebriated crowd enjoying their evening around him – enjoyment that would rapidly dissipate once they realized the act they had come to see was not going to show up. 'They'll want their money back at the very least!'

'But is she okay?'

'What?' He frowned. 'Oh yes, she'll survive. But they've taken her to Casualty. What am I going to do?'

'Do you want *me* to go on?' I heard the words as if someone else was speaking them. To this day, I don't know what possessed me.

It was an opportunity and I seized it.

As I rounded the corner of the street (the street which I have never left since that day), I heaved an enormous sigh of relief to see it empty of any signs of life except a large ginger cat trying to climb onto an overflowing wheelie bin. To the untrained eye, this little cul-de-sac looked like nothing more than a collection of rear entrances to warehouses.

My fears about the press having tracked Roni down here were unfounded, but wouldn't have been if she had had her way with the magazine shoots and made its whereabouts known to the press. This would have made my plan impossible, not to mention destroying one of this apartment's chief assets: its disguise as a grubby warehouse. 'Appearances can deceive, Danny boy, especially when they're meant to.' Iris gave me strength as I found a dark doorway opposite and prepared myself to wait until after dark. If

Roni was there, I would be able to see lights going on. If she wasn't, I could put the first stage of my plan into action. The only way forward was to take one step at a time.

That night in the East End pub many years earlier, following my bold and impulsive offer to perform being accepted, I realized I had to put an act together very rapidly from the material and soundtracks at my disposal. Ironically, the restrictions made the task easier by limiting my choices. Ten minutes later, following a less than hearty introduction from the promoter himself (whom I later found out promptly went and hid in the gents toilet until he heard the somewhat delayed appreciative reaction from the audience), I launched myself onto the stage to perform a hastily assembled – and largely instinctual – act involving sung impersonations of Karen Carpenter, Diana Ross, Patsy Cline and Dusty Springfield, along with a lot of improvised monologue and dialogue, including a conversation between the Queen and Margaret Thatcher about facial hair removal.

I remember that the audience were less than impressed with me (or the fact that I wasn't the comedienne they were expecting) when I stepped onto the stage. But I remember more vividly that it was this need to win them over that made me try harder. As soon as I felt the faintest wave of appreciation emanating from the formerly hostile crowd, I fed on it in order to throw something back on which they could continue to feed.

Whether I liked it or not, I had embarked on my career as a performer. Since then, my entire professional life has been spent living on my wits. I have realized that, unless I am doing so, I don't feel alive.

Two watchful hours later, once darkness had well and truly cast its flimsy blanket over the capital, I emerged from the dark doorway. I had satisfied myself that Roni wasn't in residence, unless she was wandering around an unlit apartment, which was hardly likely to be the case since she liked constant illumination except when she was sleeping. I crossed the road while delving into my bag to retrieve the set of keys. It only occurred to me at that precise moment that she might have had the locks changed.

In case you were wondering, the fat comedienne made a full recovery and went on to win a Perrier award and has enjoyed numerous television appearances since. Strangely, she gave up the sung impersonations (which were, as I said, really interpretations) and took on the dead-pan method of delivery employed by the first comic on that fateful night, who subsequently gave up comedy and became an IT specialist.

Live performance has a habit of directing performers towards the medium in which they excel rather than that in which they think they are going to be successful. So much depends on the ability to make the most of opportunities.

My fears about the locks proved, fortunately, to be ill founded. It couldn't have been called breaking in as I had the keys and knew the code to disable the burglar alarm, but I felt like an intruder as I entered the silent apartment, which I was now in no doubt would soon be owned entirely by Roni, along with Danron Productions and the sum total of our wealth.

I walked into the unlit hallway – afraid to betray my presence by putting lights on – and moved towards the main living area that was lit through its enormous windows by the light from the full moon. Our belongings, which had only been moved in the day before I flew to Italy, were still in boxes and crates. I felt as if I was trespassing on someone else's life. Or it might be more truthful to say that I felt as if I was playing a part in a reconstruction of my own life – one of those low budget true life dramas beloved of our American counterparts and small-time actors whose living they provide. But isn't that how I've felt all my life? I'm afraid to say that it is, except of course when Iris made me realize I was a worthwhile performer and consequently a useful human being. The other exception was much more recently on the journey to and arrival at the Greek villa.

I paused briefly to look out of the huge floor-to-ceiling windows – expertly framed with the newly-tailored muslin curtains edged with embroidery I had painstakingly designed myself to be made by hand in Rajasthan – at the Thames below, marvelling at the moon reflected in its murky swirling depths and wondering how, after all the planning and work that had gone into the construction of the apartment, my first chance to properly absorb this nocturnal river view could be in such strange and strained circumstances.

In retrospect, I realize that I was assuming a lot at that point, but I've often found my most productive actions have been based on mere hunches. In the Early Days, my entire performance was guided by hastily acted upon intuition as to what would elicit a favourable reaction from the audience. Now I was, once again, living on my wits.

'Ride from the seat of your pants!'

I booted up Roni's computer, which was set up and connected to the internet in the study even though the rest of the apartment was still in a state of disarray. I was used to working on the machine to send and receive the few emails I found necessary. Roni and I were set up as separate users – each password protected – and I can honestly tell you that, until that moment, it had never occurred to me to try to look at any of her documents or emails. In order to do so, I realized I would need to find her password. I glanced at my watch and wondered whether she would be coming home and, if so, at what time. The task of finding her password was one that could take all night.

Undaunted by the prospect, I typed in (unsuccessfully) the word 'talent', followed by my second (also unsuccessful) attempt 'fame', then – for reasons of which I am still not certain – I tried 'infamous', at which the screen changed and the machine allowed me into its cache of Roni's private dealings. It was a sign that destiny was on my side. Without a moment's hesitation and still following my instincts, I started by looking at her emails.

Any guilt I may have still harboured at invading her privacy was immediately dispelled as I scrolled through her inbox and found forwarded copies of all my personal emails, not to mention regular logs of any websites I had visited. There were, amongst them, copies of my flight details to Greece along with particulars about the rental of the villa. I now know that she was able – with the help of some readily available software – to tag all of my internet activity remarkably easily and had been doing so for some years. At the time I felt a mixture of elation that my hunch had been correct and outrage that she had impinged on the little bit of privacy I had been naïve enough to think I still possessed.

My searching was at last rewarded, as a name seemed to detach itself from the plethora of words and leap out at me from the screen. Roni had been in correspondence with Richard Dingell – the man who was, in death, to become the Body in The Pool. Of all the emails, one with 'Your Car' on the subject line drew my attention. I opened it to find a short email that read 'Invoice for your new car attached with details of where to pick it up.' The attached invoice detailed that the car – a Mini convertible – had been paid for with my credit card. I scrolled down to another email entitled 'Flight Details'. I wasn't surprised at this point to find an attached e-ticket in Richard Dingell's name to the Greek airport at which I had landed. The plot was unfolding.

I had just opened an email outlining instructions for him to collect a thermos flask – the contents of which were no doubt the product of that seemingly spontaneous night of passion in the guest suite – when my investigations were brought to an abrupt halt by sounds indicating Roni's arrival home. It was her laugh I heard first, then a car door slam. As quick as a flash, I shut down the computer, dashed to the front door to reset the alarm and hid, remembering to take the small bag containing my passport and money with me, in a large built-in cupboard in the hallway. My heart was beating so loudly that I was worried Roni would be able to hear it, but I pacified myself with the fact that she wouldn't be listening for it; as far as she was concerned, I was safely under supervision at the palazzo in Italy.

The door opened and I heard the alarm code being punched in. 'God, I need a drink!' Her heels clicked on the limestone floor, followed by another set of softer footsteps. She wasn't alone. 'Do you want one darling?' The sound of her heels clicking receded in volume as she walked through to the kitchen. I heard the fridge door open. 'Rex? What do you want to drink?' I hadn't bargained or allowed for her having anyone with her. My heart threatened to leap out of my chest as it beat more loudly still. Adrenalin rushed through my system. There was more than the satisfaction of an audience at stake here.

'Alcohol's not going to make this go away, you know.' Rex sounded concerned.

'Don't even begin to think about telling me I can't have a drink!' Roni snapped. 'Do you want vodka or gin?'

'Look, darling,' Rex was trying a softer approach, 'don't you think you should just go to bed? This has all been a terrible shock.' I heard ice cubes clinking into a glass and the gentle 'glug, glug' of liquid being poured. 'Roni! Drinking's not going to help!' I heard the glass being slammed down on a hard surface and more liquid being poured. 'You need a clear head to face the press again tomorrow.' No response came from Roni, just the 'glug, glug' of more alcoholic spirit followed by a prolonged period of silence. I could picture her draining her glass defiantly. The look in her eyes would tell him that nobody tried to tell Veronica Bedford what to do without regretting it.

'Rex, why don't you just fuck off and stick to what you do best?' Her voice was tinged with venom. 'Unless, that is, you've genuinely fallen for my wounded wife routine.' The venom had become scorn. A whimper followed by a sob indicated – to my experienced ears – that she had suddenly realized she may have gone too far and needed to get him back on her side.

'I know you're tough, Roni, but this is too much for you to deal with on your own.' There was the distinctive sound of clinking glass again and a dismissive sigh from Roni. 'You can't keep this act up you know.' I could imagine Rex walking over and putting a hand on her shoulder as he looked at her seemingly stricken form. Roni: the wronged wife and betrayed manager, enduring her ordeal with the stoicism of Joan of Arc. She would be able to fool Rex because he would have no idea what she had really done.

Rex Avalon, who was used to the evil and twisted machinations of the celebrity world, was apparently well and truly convinced by the full-throttle acting of Veronica Bedford. The poor fool no doubt even believed that she was bravely hiding her personal grief and torment behind her tough visage and harsh words. Layer upon layer of deceit. How seldom appearance and reality coincide in the private lives of those whose living depends on the two being mistaken for each other.

She clearly had Rex exactly where she wanted him. And she would use his belief in her mercilessly. Unless she was stopped. 'He's eating out of the palm of her hand, Danny boy, just like you were. You know what you've got to do!' I could hear the words as if Iris was alive and in the cupboard with me, rather than dead and in my head.

I heard Roni pour another drink. At least I assumed it was Roni pouring a drink rather than Rex, because I then heard him clear his throat to speak. 'Are you going to be alright here on your own? Do you want me to stay?' There was a pause during which, I imagine, she was draining her glass again.

'Of course I'm going to be alright on my own!' The decision to curb her harsh derision had clearly been forgotten. The effect of the alcohol was causing her to slur her words slightly. 'I hope you're not getting sympathetic on me Rex!' And then she laughed – a haunting, high-pitched cackle that gave me the same sudden urgent need to urinate I used to get when my mother shouted at me when I was veering out of control on horseback (her disapproval ranking higher than the clear dangers posed by my saddle-bound predicament). 'Sympathy,' she spat, spacing out the next few words to emphasize them, 'is – no – fucking – use – to – any – body!'

'Look, Roni, I think you've had enough to drink.' Rex sounded genuinely sympathetic and, while marvelling at his patience, I knew the unintended effect it would have.

'Go to hell!' The venom in her words was very nearly palpable. 'I'm not one of your pointless stupid little celebrities who's got herself into a bit of a pickle!'

'I'll overlook that remark,' he sounded offended, 'and come back to see you tomorrow.' He didn't put into words his sentiment that by then the effects of the alcohol would have worn off and she might be more amenable. He didn't need to.

'There you go again!' Roni's voice came from further away. She must have walked over to the far side of the room. I pictured her rolling out her arms for dramatic effect with the London skyline as her backdrop. 'You're patronizing me with your fucking empty sympathy! Do I need sympathy, Rex? Am I a victim? Is that how you see me?'

'Whether you like it or not, you *are* a victim – a victim of Danny's stupid and reckless—'

'Ha!' Her exclamation coincided with a glass smashing on the floor, no doubt a deliberate ploy to dramatize her outburst. 'That's where you're wrong, Rex. That's where you're so delightfully wrong!' Her heels clicked on the wooden floor. She was positioning herself for the next line. 'The mighty Rex Avalon fooled by the underestimated but soon-to-be-great Veronica Bedford!'

'Roni, I'm going to leave now before you say anything you might regret. For God's sake, even you couldn't come up with a body in a swimming pool on demand!' He sounded eager to leave. I detected more than a hint of fear in his voice. Was it fear of what she might admit to?

'Go on then, Rex, run off home.' She laughed again. 'You can't cope with not being able to advise on a situation, can you?'

'Roni, you've been under a lot of pressure. You need to calm down and get some sleep.'

'Rex, my darling, *you* need to refrain from offering me sympathetic advice unless I ask for it.' Her voice followed his footsteps, which were coming towards my hiding place as he beat a hasty retreat towards the door. 'Which, incidentally, will be *never*!' The door slammed shut and I knew he had gone. If my rapidly emerging plan worked, Rex Avalon had quite likely seen the last of Veronica Bedford for a very long time.

Silence fell on the apartment for what seemed like hours and I began to wonder if Roni had passed into an alcohol-induced stupor on one of the sofas. If she had, would it be safe for me to emerge from my hiding place? If I did, what was I going to do next? My dilemma was solved when I heard her stir, followed by her heels clicking first on the wooden floor, then on the stone steps leading up to the guest suite. I counted the clicks as I envisaged her progress up the stairs. Halfway up, the clicking abruptly ceased. My breathing stopped along with it – involuntarily of course – then started again as the clicking resumed, decreasing in volume as I pictured Roni reaching the top of the stairs. The guest suite had evidently been her domain since my departure, since the night she had lured me there to perform the act which I now knew was an essential detail in the intricate plot she had been hatching.

At last, the boot was on the other foot. I had been dancing to her tune for too long; now it was her turn to dance to mine. The monkey was about to change places with the organ grinder.

'You should wait until the bitch is asleep, then creep in there and strangle her!' Stella's advice was as welcome as it was helpful. I wanted to ask her why she was suddenly siding with me against Roni when her support, which would certainly have been welcome, was noticeably absent during my incarceration in Greece. 'Don't tell me she doesn't deserve it!' I couldn't disagree, but had other plans for my wife. As Iris would have said – and often did – 'There are more ways than one to skin a cat, Danny boy!'

The food delivery man has just left. Tonight, I engaged him in quite a long chat, which he probably found uncharacteristic. It was mainly about the freshness of the fillet steak and the quality of the foie gras he had brought. He didn't see me of course, but he still chatted away through the intercom, asking if I had a dinner party planned. 'Yes,' was the response, 'tomorrow is going to be a big day.'

'Goodnight then, madam. Nice talking to you.' Even though I have never met him face to face, I'm going to miss his deferential dependability.

When I eventually emerged from the cupboard, having waited in its dark confines for longer than was probably necessary, I was still attentive to the slightest sound that would betray the fact that Roni was awake. I took off my shoes to minimize the noise my progress would make and crossed the living room one step at a time, looking furtively up at the barred windows above me. Behind their Victorian glass panes, she was hopefully fast asleep.

I put my foot on the bottom step, knowing that this ascension marked the crossing of the point of no return. My other foot felt for the second step in the dark and I suddenly realized that the point in question had been crossed long before, although not by me. Unless I was going to give in and prolong my role as victim, I had little choice but to continue on my chosen course of action.

Slowly, stealthily, I reached the top step and let my fingers trace the contours of the heavy open door that, when closed, would separate the guest suite from the rest of the apartment. I tiptoed into the dark bedroom from where I could hear the sound of my wife snoring loudly. In the near total darkness I could barely make out her supine form on the large bed, but I knew she would be lying on her back with her mouth open. A pillow – which she had evidently cast aside in her drunken progress to bed – was on the floor. I moved quietly towards it and picked it up.

My act in the Early Days developed quite steadily and was formed around my mimicry and impersonations, which had proved so successful as part of my debut performance. Using swift costume changes and numerous incidental props, I found that my repertoire grew at an alarming rate.

Stella's first appearance occurred a couple of years later. As I've already explained, I knew from the outset that she was different. She even dictated the wig, costumes and make-up I needed to give physical form to her being. Having allowed her to live and breathe on stage, I had given birth to the first woman in my life to dictate what I should or shouldn't do. From that time forward, Stella Finkelstein – the Bermondsey Bombshell – was part of my life for ever.

Holding the pillow in my hand, I looked down at Roni's sleeping form. 'Go on! Smother the bitch!' I was glad that Stella's strident words could only be heard by me. 'She deserves it!' I still can't say for certain whether or not I was tempted to follow her advice, but I am proud to say that – if I was – I resisted. My eyes, by now accustomed to the darkness, scanned the room for Roni's handbag and found it by the foot of the bed.

Opening it, I saw the blue glow from her mobile phone. I closed the handbag again and grasped it under my left arm. So far, so good.

Still moving slowly and quietly, ever mindful of the pattern of Roni's breathing, I knelt down to unplug the phone that sat on the bedside cabinet and gently picked it up, careful not to let the receiver fall off and wake her. Laden with the handbag and the telephone, I backed out of the bedroom into the tiny hallway, then past the heavy door and out onto the stairway, putting the handbag down so that I could carefully take the key from the lock on the inside.

The door swung closed with barely a sound thanks to the thorough restoration of the old cast iron hinges I had diligently overseen. I put the key into the keyhole and used both hands to turn it, no longer bothering to attempt to be quiet as the three mortise locks slid home with a rasp of metal on metal. I shuddered inwardly as I was reminded of the iron door of the Greek prison cell being closed on my bewildered misery. Now the roles had been well and truly reversed. Roni was my prisoner as I had been hers for years.

My outfit for tonight's Night Delivery is a sharply-cut Balmain suit Roni wore for a meeting with the press – accompanied by Rex – on the day I was released from the Greek prison and sent back to Italy. I saw photos of her wearing it in several newspapers. It will be the basis for a stoical 'wronged wife' look that comprises a pale face seemingly devoid of make-up (although this look actually requires more time and cosmetic assistance than a radiant on-top-of-the-world look) and ash blonde hair drawn back tightly into a bun at the back of the head. It's a look, Stella says, suitable for attending the funeral of a loved one. What would she know? It could be said that she doesn't know anything unless I let her, in the same way that it could be theorized that she can't say anything unless I allow her to. But that – I am sure you have realized by now – is not true.

What is tonight's Night Delivery thinking? By that, I mean specifically right at this moment rather than generally. There is, of course, the chance that he will change his mind. I somehow know, though, that he won't. I have confidence in the fact that I have allowed for every eventuality. My forearm is throbbing from the small elaborate 'R' I tattooed on it earlier. He won't feel the effects of the larger version of the same letter I will imprint on his chest later, since his nerve endings will no longer be sending messages to his brain by then. He will – I fervently hope – be at peace.

Will I ever find a similar peace? Is that the purpose of this memoir? Will it be my legacy or will it never be read? While in this questioning mode, it could be asked whether I am recording facts for posterity, simply putting over my version of events, or writing this in an attempt to preserve my sanity.

Imprisoned

D

With Roni now locked in the guest suite – which had been designed as a haven of privacy, but fortunately for me served equally well as a prison – I descended the stone stairs and felt able, for the first time since my return to the apartment, to linger over and really enjoy the view of the river below and the sprawling metropolis beyond.

Now, two years, three hundred and fifty-seven days later, I look down at the same river and wonder whether I can accurately remember what was going through my mind on that night. The river looks much the same as it did then, even though the water of which it is comprised has changed many times in the intervening days; it is a reconstruction of the river that rippled darkly below me on that night. Does that make it any more or less genuine (it is, after all, still very much the River Thames) than this retrospective account of my feelings? Perhaps it would be safer for me to adhere to an account of my actions. I know I looked down at the murky swirling water for a long time – perhaps an hour or even more – before strolling at a curiously leisurely pace around this space that I had created and furnished. I suppose, however fanciful it may sound now, I felt like an exiled monarch returning to his kingdom. And once again I find myself writing about my feelings.

It would, no doubt, be advisable to return immediately to reporting my physical movements, leaving my thoughts and feelings in my memory where they belong. But not before sharing the thought that has been recurring a lot lately: that I will miss this solitary existence of mine, but have to be realistic about the fact that it is about to come to an end.

Before long, on that night that seems alternately a lifetime away and also as if it could have been just a few days ago, I hurried to Roni's study and switched on her computer, ready to take up where I had left off abruptly at her return. It was still springing to digital life when the mobile phone rang. I rushed to the bottom of the stairs where I had left the handbag, tipped its contents onto the polished wooden floor, grabbed the phone and answered it, instinctively eager to preserve the silence.

'Hello?' I had the equally intuitive presence of mind to use Roni's voice.

'Signora Bedford?' It was a voice with a heavy Italian accent. 'This is Silvio Cescutti from Palazzo Gridolfo.' I knew what the call was about, but Roni wouldn't have. 'Signora Bedford? Are you there?'

'Of course I'm here!' I slurred her words just slightly. If she had been awake, she would have been displaying signs of intoxication. 'What do you want?' I stood up and walked to look at the river again, praising myself for having retrieved the handbag and the mobile it contained from the guest suite.

'Your 'usband is not 'ere.' He sounded nervous.

'What do you mean he isn't there?' I made the question angrily terse, giving him a reason for his nervousness.

'The room is empty, Signora. I think 'e 'as left.'

'Well, perhaps your hospitality wasn't to his liking!'

'There is the small matter of the bill—'

'Oh for God's sake!' I didn't like to be so brusque with the man, but was still in character. 'Send the bloody bill to me here in London if that's all you're worried about!'

'Very well, Signora. Please remember I am only doing what you asked me to do.'

'I know.' I made her voice soften slightly. 'Please forgive me. You can't imagine the pressure I've been under.' I was aware – and indeed hoped – that this conversation might be being documented.

'Good night Signora.' The call ended and I went back to the computer to continue my investigations.

I am wearing the clothes in which I travelled back from Italy. The Levi's jeans and Abercrombie and Fitch T-shirt haven't been washed since that day. I've been saving them for tonight.

After the instructions about the thermos flask and its contents, I couldn't find any more emails between Roni and Richard Dingell. How on earth had she found him? More to the point, how had she persuaded him to travel to Greece, inseminate himself then commit suicide? Was a new car valuable enough to trade for a life? I was still puzzling over the facts and my inability to grasp the entire picture when it occurred to me to look at her web activity.

The moment I saw the list of websites she had visited, I knew I was more than one step closer to finding the truth. Among them were several sites dealing with methods of suicide (including a Japanese one detailing how toilet cleaner could be mixed with pesticide to make a cloud of deadly hydrogen sulphide gas), two intended to support people involved with or contemplating being involved with assisted suicide and a site run by an organization calling itself 'Suicide is Painless' with a live chat room. This, I had a hunch, was where she had found Richard Dingell. On further investigation, I found that the computer had saved a log-in name and password. The log-in name was – eerily – 'DannyD'. Just as I was about to enter the chat room, the phone on the desk rang. The caller display helpfully told me it was Rodney Markham. I picked up the receiver.

'Hello?'

'Roni, it's Rodney.'

'I know.' I was more than well acquainted with my wife's terse telephone manner.

'To put it succinctly, you were right about the DNA sample taken from the body matching Danny's.'

'I knew it!' Roni, I felt, would show some satisfaction at having been right, even if it confirmed that her husband was having a homosexual affair. Or, at least, that is how she would want it to appear to her lawyer.

'So all of Danny's assets are now yours.' He paused. 'That is, if you want me to go ahead with—'

'Of course I want you to go ahead with it, Rodney!'

'I just wanted to be sure it was what you wanted.'

'It is.' I made Roni heave a sigh of resignation. 'And it might be pertinent to let the family of the dead man know that my husband has no assets whatsoever.'

'Of course.'

'I know I can rely on you to handle it, Rodney.' With that I prepared to dismiss him. 'I'm a very busy woman, as you know, and don't want to be bothered any more. Goodbye.' I put the receiver down before he had time to answer and turned my concentration back to the computer screen in front of me. Now it had been confirmed that my sperm was present in the Body in The Pool, I knew I was correct about the contents of the thermos flask. Roni's tearful entreaties for me to sleep with her on that first night in this apartment had clearly been as calculated and premeditated as virtually every move she had made since we had met. However far-fetched it sounded, she had succeeded. But now she was locked in the guest suite and I was in control.

I entered the chat room on the 'Suicide is Painless' site and found that there were fifteen other people logged in. Taking a few moments to figure out how it was structured, I looked at the three messages in my (or was it Roni's) inbox.

'*How much are you offering?*' read the first.

'*I am interested in your offer,*' said the second.

'*Please reply – I am at the end of my tether but need to leave my family some money.*' It was this third one that began to make sense.

That night I went to bed for the first time in my new bedroom – the room that had been designed as 'our' bedroom. Considering how my mind must have been racing, I distinctly remember that I slept rather soundly, waking well after sunrise with the feeling that, as my plan was taking shape and developing, I was genuinely capable of bringing it to a satisfactory conclusion.

I came through the heavy curtains onto the iron walkway and looked down with approval onto the apartment below me. Sunlight was filtering through the flimsy muslin drawn across the floor-to-ceiling windows, making patterns on the old polished floorboards, highlighting the patina of age that told so many stories both real and imagined. I descended the stairs slowly, enjoying the reality of this private space that, without me, wouldn't be in existence in its present form. Gently opening one set of curtains, I gazed down at the Thames below. The boats going past in both directions fascinated me, each with its individual function. One in particular drew my attention: a small tug boat pulling two barges stacked with large yellow freight containers. I could see the man steering it. He had his purpose. And I had mine.

The first task I had set myself was to organize the apartment by unpacking the boxes and crates piled up where the removal men had left them. I had been quite meticulous about organizing what we did and didn't bring to our new home, so I knew everything would have a place. Looking back, the action of putting everything in its designated position, bringing order to the former chaos around me, was an essential step in getting my mind clearly focussed on the task ahead. The phone rang a few times, but I let the callers be dealt with by the answering service, unwilling to be swayed from my work.

At around nine o'clock, I heard a noise from the guest suite, followed by a loud hammering on the inside of the door. Roni, it seemed, had woken up and discovered that she was locked in. I remember that I was quite calm. Of course, it is possible that I am altering my remembered feelings to match my subsequently acquired knowledge that the suite was quite capable of resisting her attempts to escape. Either way, I had little to worry about since she was securely incarcerated. The steel-framed windows overlooking the living area, which I have since covered up with heavy tapestries, were never designed to open. The door was heavier and stronger than that on a prison cell. The small lift, which was the only other link between my space and hers, was too small for her to climb into, but provided me with a means of feeding her.

The door hasn't been opened since that night I closed and bolted it after a glance at her sleeping form. Thus, I haven't had to come face-to-face with my wife in all that time – unless, of course, you can count the numerous occasions when looking in the mirror prior to the Night Deliveries.

That first day, I made her wait for her food until well into the afternoon. I haven't done that since, probably because of a nagging fear that I would get to enjoy being her jailer. Aside from the odd frisson of wicked pleasure derived from giving her food I know she won't want to eat but will be too hungry to refuse, I have tried to keep my role purely functional.

By the end of that day, the apartment was looking very nearly as good as I had hoped and dreamed it would. My risks – using wildly opposing materials in close conjunction with each other in the hope of creating a discordant harmony – had all worked without exception. I hadn't, in any area or detail, gone for the easy option and the results spoke for themselves. I suppose that this evident success and resulting feeling of elation spurred me on to be more daring with my plan: this intricate web of revenge that is nearing its conclusion. Will it be a success? I truly don't know. But isn't that what makes it so brilliant? I like to think so. Right up to the last moment, it is as likely to fail as it is to succeed.

Tonight's letter is a 'D' I found in a Latin bible (circa 1653) bearing the arms of Louis XIV on its faded Morocco gilt binding. The letter is from the book of Exodus, which I find rather fitting. I have already tattooed it on my right forearm, so the legend is complete – 'VERONICA' on my left arm, 'BEDFORD' on my right. The larger version of the 'D' on my chest is going to be more difficult and much more painful.

It had been a long and physically strenuous day and, by seven o'clock in the evening, I felt fully justified in settling down on one of the grey leather Chesterfield sofas with a large glass of Pinot Grigio while I listened to the telephone messages that had been left during the course of the day. Roni, it transpired, had missed two meetings with a producer at the television company with which she had been negotiating over the New Show. I decided to take the bull by the horns and call back immediately.

'Good Morning. Hen's Teeth Productions!' The receptionist sounded cheerful and I paused briefly to envy her evident contentment.

'This is Veronica Bedford from Danron.' I chose an imperious tone. 'I need to leave a message for Steve Bernstein.'

'I'll put you through to his office now, Miss Bedford.' I waited for several minutes, no doubt employing more patience than Roni would have.

'Steve Bernstein's office.'

'This is Veronica Bedford.'

'Ah, Miss Bedford, Mr Bernstein has been trying to call you.'

'I know.' I paused for effect. 'Can you please tell him that I have severe reservations about his proposal? I will call him when I have had time to think about it,' I paused again, 'and not before. Kindly inform him that it would be unwise to bother me in the meantime.' I replaced the receiver, unable to suppress a smile.

Needless to say, I treated all his subsequent calls and emails in a similar manner. I am possibly mistaken in my memories, but am reasonably certain that I gained a considerable amount of enjoyment from impersonating Roni in those days when my plan, The Plan, was in its infancy. Each call was a fresh challenge, a new challenge, a step on which I may have fallen down.

'Roni!' Rex sounded relieved and apprehensive at the same time. 'How do you feel this morning?'

'Fine!' I didn't want to arouse his suspicion by making her pleasant. 'Why shouldn't I be?'

'No reason.' He was a bad liar. 'Shall I come over?'

'Of course not!' I brought more than a hint of derision into her tone. 'I can manage this on my own, thank you.'

'So why did you call?' He sounded confused.

'To tell you that I can manage on my own, of course!' I replaced the receiver.

I cancelled all her appointments – without giving convincing reasons for doing so – and slowly and systematically contacted The Friends and The Acquaintances, ostensibly to inform them that Roni had no need of their help and support. It is still a source of amusement to me, all this time later, to picture their reactions.

The Novelist, Alan McBeigh, whose only contact with Roni in years had been at our second wedding must have been completely bewildered, along with

Jonathan and Rowena English, Shaun Kettering and Melanie Threadgold. They could all have been forgiven for thinking that she was – through denial – seeking their help. I had fun with Neil Ashcroft, giving him a hint that his knowledge of production techniques – albeit in commercials rather than actual programmes – might be useful, before letting him know that it wouldn't be.

I dislike myself for it, but I had fun.

Nothing is more effective in making people feel that they could be useful than telling them that their help is not required.

The most enjoyable call by far was the one I made to Ellie Franklin. Of all The Friends, she was the one who – in my opinion – most needed to be put in her place. I felt like a screenwriter engineering a scene he has been postponing in order to savour its creation. From Roni's emails, I had discovered that Ellie had decided to branch out from representing sports personalities and was making plans to broaden her horizons into the even more competitive world of actors and singers. Roni had involved her in the proposed New Show from the early stages. The implication was clearly that Ellie would have the opportunity of managing any of the 'Natural Talent' discovered, along with an all-important credit on the titles. Regardless of the fact that I knew the show wasn't going to go ahead, I wanted to tell Ellie what I thought of her. Or, to be more precise, I wanted Roni to tell her what she thought of her.

'Ellie darling!'

'Roni! How the devil are you?' Ellie's gushing superior tone irritated me as much as usual.

'I wanted you to know that Danron is now completely mine, darling.'

'Fabulous news!'

'I'm going it alone from now on.' I made Roni sound positive and in control.

'You can do it, darling. And you know I'll be with you every step of the way.'

'Well, sweetie, that's actually why I'm ringing.' Now Roni's voice contained a hint of apology.

'Really?' Ellie had picked it up and was clearly worried.

'The thing is...' I paused theatrically and listened to Ellie taking a deep breath at the other end of the line. I made the silence last for a few more delicious seconds. 'The thing is, darling,' I paused again and pictured her agonized expression, her hands fumbling with the silk scarf around her neck, 'to be brutally frank, I'm not sure you're up to the task.'

'What?' Ellie's practised method of elocution was momentarily forgotten.

'You see, I can't afford to invest any more time and energy in something that's going to be thrown back in my face.' I made Roni speak slowly and clearly. Her intention – I felt – would be to maximize the impact of her words by being patronizing. 'Danny's behaviour has knocked me for six and has brought the memories of my mother's lack of—'

'How dare you compare me with your bloody mother?' Ellie sounded delightfully angry.

'I wasn't,' I made Roni pause again, 'but since you mention it, there could be similarities.'

'So you don't want to be associated with me in case I don't live up to your expectations?' Ellie's words were tumbling out. 'What would you do if I didn't? Kill me too?'

'How dare you!' I spat Roni's retort back at her.

'So you're going to deny it then?' Ellie was clearly on a roll and not about to hold back. I could see that I was going to learn something. 'You want me to conveniently forget what you told me?'

'I told you in confidence!' The strident words hid my curiosity.

'But that doesn't alter the fact that you told me, does it?' Ellie's tone was now menacing. 'How do you think it would look if it accidentally got out that you had helped your mother to commit suicide?' She paused. 'Oh, silly me, it can't really have been suicide, can it, when she didn't want to die?'

'You'd better not be threatening me!' I sincerely hoped that she was. 'It would be your word against mine.'

'Oh, darling, I don't think there would be much doubt surrounding the matter if I drew attention to your having seen yourself through two very expensive years at drama school with your inheritance.'

'You fucking bitch!' I slammed the receiver down hard and took a deep breath. While I had suspected – from the conflicting stories she had told me – that there was something strange about the demise of her mother, I wouldn't have believed that Roni was actually capable of killing her. More chilling was the fact that she had no doubt justified the deed in her own mind by convincing herself that her mother's life was worth nothing because she had given up on her career.

Needless to say, a considerable period of time passed before Ellie Franklin attempted to get in touch with Roni again. When she did, my impression of her as a ruthless professional with no need for real friends was confirmed. I could see what they saw in each other.

The dining table, which is actually an enormous door suspended on cables – will be laid this evening for nine people. It is the first time this has been done, the first time it will be used for its intended purpose. I am going to give myself plenty of time to do it in order to pay attention to every last detail. Place cards – ordered by post from a recommended calligrapher in Hampstead – arrived last week. I know that some of the guests won't turn up, but the important thing is that they have been invited.

There will be no Night Delivery tonight. Instead, as I have told you, the last letter will be tattooed on my own body. The final Tattooed Body. The time is drawing closer and, as always, timing is of the utmost importance. Soon I will be unlocking that door that has stood between my wife and me for the last two years, three hundred and fifty seven days. Will she show remorse? Will she express understanding? Will her reactions prove that I have completely underestimated her? Whatever her reaction will be, the fact remains that I have set the wheels in motion and there is no turning back.

Her freshly dry-cleaned outfit has been sent up in the lift. I hope she makes an effort with her appearance for her return to the world outside the guest suite. Even though I am dreading it, I am now counting the minutes until it is time to unlock the door.

Along with numerous stories – both spoken and printed – that Veronica Bedford is leading a reclusive existence in her riverside apartment, many have also surfaced about *my* alleged whereabouts. I have, according to undisclosed sources, been spotted living a quiet way of life in locations ranging from a Portuguese monastery to a remote villa in Sardinia.

The Escape

I am in excruciating pain!

When the time came, I ascended the stairs to the guest suite. My actions were not, I might add, executed without a great deal of trepidation. Each step brought me closer to the success or failure of The Plan. The locks on the heavy door slid back as I turned the key. That was just a few minutes ago. Now I am sitting on the floor of the bedroom in the guest suite writing this with my right hand and nursing a quite serious head wound with my left. I am locked in. *She* locked me in. Roni's prison has become mine.

Despite harbouring what I saw as realistic expectations, I wasn't ready for her to resort to such immediate and spontaneous violence. The chair came crashing down on my head the split second I opened the door. She had evidently been waiting for this moment. I can't help but admire her ability – throughout the long days and nights – to cling on to the belief that I would sooner or later unlock the portal of her incarceration. Belief, after all, is the backbone of existence. She believed and she was ready.

There was no antagonistic greeting. No 'What the fuck have you been playing at?' No 'What the bloody hell's going on?' Just a heavy Gothic Revival hall chair crashing down on my head, causing me to lose consciousness, albeit momentarily.

Now I must hurry to hide this memoir away from prying eyes.

What the Newspapers Said...

Daily Mail   June 10th
'Celebrity questioned over Tattooed Thames Bodies
A late night police presence at the luxury London apartment of shamed television star Danny Devereux was rumoured to be in connection with the series of tattooed bodies found floating in the Thames over the last two weeks...'

The Times   June 10th
'Danny Devereux linked to mystery of Tattooed Bodies
Police were called last night to the Thames-side apartment of Veronica Bedford, best known as the wife of television host Danny Devereux...'

Daily Mirror   June 10th
'Police swoop on celebrities in lead on Tattoo Killer
Amidst a celebrity-studded dinner party, police swooped on the luxury Thames-side apartment of Veronica Bedford and Danny Devereux last night. Publicist to the stars Rex Avalon said, in a brief statement, "I had no idea what was going on. I arrived as a dinner guest and was understandably shocked to discover that someone I saw as

a friend could be implicated in such a series of horrifying crimes."

Devereux (38) has been missing from public life for three years since a body tattooed with his name was found floating in the swimming pool of a Greek villa he was renting, giving rise to allegations that he was leading a secret drug-fuelled gay life. Bedford (43), who was credited with engineering his meteoric rise to fame, has been living as a recluse in the London apartment during that time.

Agent to the stars Ellie Franklin (46) was also present at the apartment. "I hadn't seen Roni for some time as a result of a professional rift. Being invited to dinner was almost as surprising as what we found when we got there.'"

The Sun   June 11th
'Celebrity Couple refuse to comment on Tattooed Murders

Film actor Shaun Kettering and his soap star wife Melanie Threadgold, currently the subjects of speculation over personal and professional turmoil, shied away from reporters following the revelation that they were invited to the Thames-side apartment on the night of the sensational arrest.

Claiming they were "no longer close" with Danny Devereux and Veronica Bedford, whose idyllic wedding they hosted a number of years ago at their sumptuous £5m country mansion, they allegedly expressed incredulity at their invitation to the dinner. Kettering (44) is rumoured to have been romantically linked with Bedford (43) in the past.'

Evening Standard   June 17th
'Celebrity charged with Tattooed Thames Murders
Veronica Bedford, best known as wife and manager of television host Danny Devereux, was charged earlier today with fourteen counts of assisting suicide and a further charge of holding her husband captive against his will. Police arrived at her London apartment late on the night of June 9th following a call from close friend and publicist Rex Avalon.

Devereux (38) had been noticeably absent from public life since the discovery of a body floating in the swimming pool of a Greek villa in which he was staying, but was reported to have been living abroad.

Bedford (43) was arrested in front of a group of her close friends, who had apparently just arrived at her home for a dinner party. Among them was award-winning novelist Alan McBeigh. Despite the circumstances of the charges against Bedford resembling the tangled plot of one of his best-selling novels, McBeigh (49) refused to comment on Bedford's arrest. It is rumoured that he was romantically linked with her more than a decade ago, but he declined to comment.'

The Sun   June 18th

'Agent to the stars admits she knew Bedford was "evil"

Ellie Franklin (46) spoke frankly yesterday about the sorrow she feels at not having spoken sooner about suspicions that her former close friend Veronica 'Roni' Bedford (43), who was yesterday charged with fourteen counts of assisting suicide. "She confessed to me more than five years ago that she had killed her own mother in order to pay her drama school fees with the resulting inheritance." She lowered her beautifully coiffed blonde head in shame as she continued. "If I had thought for one moment that she was serious about these claims, I would have done something about it and, who knows, might have been able to avoid the reign of terror that resulted." She wiped a tear from her eye and shook her head. "Fourteen men lost their lives so that Roni could satisfy her sick desire to have her name in the headlines. I had no idea how unstable she was. The scariest thing is that she seemed to think she had done nothing wrong. That woman is the embodiment of evil."

When asked about her much-reported professional association with Bedford, Franklin sadly recounted the breakdown of their collaboration on a planned television show. "I poured a wealth of experience into that show, but am afraid that Roni's need to be in the limelight made working together completely impossible." She remained pensive about the future. "If it wasn't for the fact that many hardworking actors, singers and personalities are reliant on me to make their living, I would be seriously tempted to give up." Another tear ran down her immaculately made-up cheek. "Perhaps throwing myself whole-heartedly into my work will help me live with the guilt. Who knows?"

Comment *page 32* **Are drama school fees too high?'**

The Guardian (Arts Supplement) June 27th

'Melanie Threadgold, still in possession of her famously sylph-like figure and golden blonde hair, spoke quietly as she told of her mixture of sorrow and excitement at leaving the soap "The Other Half" in which she has had a leading role for the last nine years. "It was clearly time for me to leave," she says with a flash of her famous smile, "and I'm terribly excited about my future projects." She declined to comment on the identity of any of these, however, apart from a period drama on Channel 5, but was eager to emphasize that it had nothing to do with the rather public embarrassment involving a drunken appearance on a late night discussion programme by her film actor husband Shaun Kettering. "I'm afraid Shaun and I have decided to go our separate ways," she said with a sad shake of her Patrician head. "He is a very damaged person and, I'm afraid, his destructive behaviour stems from his relationship with the now notoriously evil Veronica Bedford."

Asked why, in this case, she still agreed to host the much-publicized wedding of Bedford and Danny Devereux, she shook her head again, perhaps more sadly this time. "It was all part of the publicity machine, I'm afraid. We were coerced into it by a publicist we have since realized feeds off the misfortunes of hard-working celebrities."'

The Guardian (Arts Supplement) July 4th

'Rex Avalon, who took time out from his hectic schedule to organize the fundraising dinner for "Hope in Hell" – the charity devoted to helping victims of bipolarity in the Arts, expressed sorrow and regret at his inability to help his long-term friend Veronica Bedford at a time when she clearly needed him. "My guilt is something I will have to learn to live with," he said sadly, "but I am no stranger to the fact that those in the public eye are susceptible to depression and insecurity. It is in their nature to need to be fully occupied all of the time."'

* * *

I could show you more of the newspaper reports, but they all recount different versions of the same events: the police – alerted by a call from Rex, who had just received a call from a distressed and repentant Roni (or so he thought) on his mobile while on the way to the apartment – arrived right on cue at the same time as the other Friends and Acquaintances who had been unable to resist turning up for the dinner party to which they thought they had been invited by Roni.

A bewildered, agitated and very vocal Roni played the part in which I had cast her, exceeding even my expectations as I hammered loudly on the inside of the door of the guest suite and alerted the police to my presence. I had gone a little overboard, perhaps, wearing clothes that hadn't been washed for three years, but the newly-tattooed 'D' on my chest, along with my hysterically tearful gratitude at being released in what appeared to be the nick of time, did the trick.

Roni's demented protestations of innocence fell on deaf ears.

The rest, as they say, is history.

Although Roni faced the charges against her, it looks as if she will be sectioned thanks to an extensive psychologist's report (which detailed her need for control and fame which led to her need to spell out her name on the dead bodies) and, as a consequence, will not have to stand trial. Either way, she will be incarcerated – almost certainly without appeal – for the rest of her life.

Meanwhile, I am contemplating my freedom and looking forward to a life of my own.

EPILOGUE

It's difficult to believe how things have turned out. Neil Ashcroft's new production company is making a film of my life, now that he has decided he is going to give up making commercials and get into the movie business. It's a ludicrous prospect, made even more bizarre by the fact that the screenplay is being written by Alan McBeigh.

Roni herself couldn't have organized it better.

Thinking about it, on the other hand, Roni would probably have organized for my part to be played by Shaun Kettering and her own by Melanie Threadgold with a film score composed by Jonathan English. Ellie Franklin would, no doubt, have been employed to handle all the rights.

I may be giving the impression of flippancy. Please do not be misled.

Stella says I should be pleased with myself, but I am not.

Jesus! Will you listen to him complaining about the way things have turned out? He says he didn't organize it, but nobody else would have had the gumption to plan, let alone the sheer daring to carry out, that charade. I still find it hard to believe that it worked, but work it did. The sneaky bugger kept the full details of what he'd got in store for that bitch Roni even from me. I'd be the first to admit I thought he'd completely lost the plot. Let's face it, he wouldn't be the first celebrity to go round the bend would he? But he hadn't. He's a genius. Too much of a genius to be kept out of the limelight.

The film came about completely spontaneously, but without me forcing him to show an interest and co-operate, he would have shied away from it. It really beggars belief, this blindness he seems to have to the potential of what's happening.

Looking back, I realize I was naïve to believe that I would be able to live in virtual anonymity, using my creative talents to make beautiful and challenging homes in which people could be themselves. It wasn't to be.

Okay, I'll admit that I did make a bit of a nuisance of myself, but it was for his own good. Unless I'd forced him to, he wouldn't have got on a stage again, let alone taken up any of the television offers.

Of course, I had to make my existence known and – to cut a long story short – the public can't get enough of me. Stella Finkelstein is now a personality in her own right. I bloody well would have been years ago if Roni hadn't got in the way!

Stella just wouldn't let me rest.

'Get out there while your name's on everyone's lips,' she said. 'They all want you now.' That's how the television offers started. Stella now hosts 'Starmaker' – a show hauntingly similar to Roni's New Show – made by a production company called 'Shooting Star Productions'. Stella is its figurehead (and I am its principal shareholder). The show gives talented but undiscovered performers a chance to get into the big time and has, so far, launched several potential stars on the road to fame and fortune. In addition, Stella appears regularly on two panel shows. There really is no stopping her. Except that, I think, some day soon I'll have to. The realization that I have escaped from the clutches of one mistress only to promptly deliver myself into the vice-like grip of another is very nearly too much to bear.

Bloody cheek! Talking about me as if I can't hear him. What does he mean 'stop me'? He might have put a stop to that viper Roni's antics, but there's no way I come into her category. I've got my sights set on the West End next. It's more than she ever did, the talentless bitch. I'll have to make sure I send her a programme.

I was a guest this evening on 'Tonight with Gerry and Lil', purely because I could no longer find a reason to refuse. It was more than a little strange to be on that sofa again after eight years. Gerry is still as smooth and tanned as ever and Lil has – in the intervening years –

married a footballer and now looks even younger than she did then.

I was – for the first time on television – completely myself and made sure I wasn't intimidated by their attempts to goad the other 'me' back into existence. They alluded to the numerous offers of chat shows that have come my way, but I declined to comment. I sensed that the interview wasn't going the way they had planned, but that was my intention. When Lil, rather too insistently for my liking, moved towards me with the clear objective of putting her hand on my arm for the kind of 'intimate' moment for which she has become famous, I allowed the sleeve of my shirt to ride up. A glimpse of the tattoos on my forearm was too much even for her. The interview, to my extreme relief, was brought to a close very soon after that.

I've done it! I've been offered the part of Widow Twankey in Aladdin at the Victoria Palace Theatre next Christmas. More to the point, I'm going to command the highest figure ever paid to a performer on the London stage – and I'm not talking just pantomime, I mean in any play or musical. What a result! I knew I could do it. I'm working every single day and still the offers keep flooding in. My public loves me!

Where will it end? You may ask, but I have just decided. It is strange to think, while I am writing this, that it is entirely possible that nobody will ever read this memoir. It is more bizarre to predict that if you (and presumably others) *are* reading these words, it is because I will have finally had enough of being slave to the second woman in my life – or maybe it would be more truthful to own up to the fact that she was always the first – and disposed of her parasitic being in the only way possible.

Is a man who chooses when to die more or less in control of his destiny than one who waits for death to take him by surprise?

ANDREW THOMAS WADLAND

KN Complete
Call 0845 0722700

ACKNOWLEDGEMENTS

I would like to thank Keith Robinson for making me fall off the back of a motorbike on Corfu, which led to this novel being conceived while my leg healed.

I am also indebted to Leonore Holder, who gave me the confidence to persevere and find Danny's voice, to Jason Dickie for supplying an authentic setting for the opening and to Paul Oxley for going the whole hog and buying the place (not to mention for reading an early manuscript at one sitting because he was 'awake until 6am anyway').

Thanks also to Anna Stolli, Ray Forder-Stent, Stephen Humphreys, James 'Biddie' Biddlecombe, Susie Doust and David Scott for feedback during the writing process.

I suppose I should also acknowledge the various performers – imaginary and real - who may or may not have inspired this work of fiction.